Jon A
march 2004

Jonathan Adams freely admits to being born and raised in the affluent township of Guildford, the county town of gin and tonic Surrey, in an era when it held the ambience of genteel living.

The daily grind of being employed within the treadmill of commerce eventually took its toll. The well-worn cliché that one was engaged in a rat race had become a reality.

He now resides in a tiny township, amidst the undulating farmland of deepest Suffolk. His life being one of therapy: frequenting the down-market, back street bars, sampling real English Ale, for which the locality is renowned, interspersed with bouts of writing idiosyncratic fiction.

FRIDAY NIGHT

Jonathan Adams

Friday Night

Chimera

CHIMERA PAPERBACK

© Copyright 2004
Jonathan Adams

The right of Jonathan Adams to be identified as author of this work has been asserted by him in accordance with the Copyright, Designs and Patents Act 1988

All Rights Reserved

No reproduction, copy or transmission of this publication may be made without written permission.
No paragraph of this publication may be reproduced, copied or transmitted save with the written permission or in accordance with the provisions
of the Copyright Act 1956 (as amended).

Any person who does any unauthorised act in relation to this publication may be liable to criminal prosecution and civil claims for damage.

A CIP catalogue record for this title is available from the British Library
ISBN 1 903136 26 1

Chimera is an imprint of
Pegasus Elliot MacKenzie Publishers Ltd.
www.pegasuspublishers.com

First Published in 2004

Chimera
Sheraton House Castle Park
Cambridge England

Printed & Bound in Great Britain

Prologue

In the heady days of our last school summer we were lovers. Her father, being somewhat sceptical of his daughter's ability to earn a living as an actress, had insisted she should obtain some respectable grades in her 'A' level examinations before he would allow her to enrol at the Drama School. For this purpose I had agreed to help her with her homework. As Head Boy at the High School, I was considered the ideal candidate for the task. The place of our study had been a summerhouse within the walled garden of her parents home.

As a 17 year old she had been outrageously extrovert, I was but a year older and somewhat bashful. My memory of events was crystal clear. The crisp white blouse of her school uniform, her pert proud breasts as she undressed before we made love on the well-cushioned wicker sun bed. Broken to womanhood, her infatuation knew no bounds. Night after night, unbeknown to our respective parents, we slept in the summerhouse.

Within a few weeks I had accepted a place at University. All too soon our summer of love had come to an end. On the few occasions I had caught sight of her about town, during my infrequent weekend visits, I had received but an aloof wave of the hand from her. Occasionally, in passing, she would greet me with a sweet and demure acknowledgement of 'Hello Benjamin, how are you? Hope you are keeping well.' Her sudden, over the top, advances in my direction had left me once again smitten.

She held a cool flamboyancy, a creature of the

evening, the band played their final rendition of the evening. A poignant blues number. On the dance floor we smooched, her arms draped about my shoulders, my hands caressing her bottom, her breasts hard against me. All the wonderful ingredients of foreplay for me to share her bed.

Discreetly slipping a folded tissue into the pocket of my jacket, with a flurry of goodbyes to her friends, she left.

Returning to the bar I ordered a whisky. Her departure had been somewhat theatrical, there was no obvious reason why we could not have left together. Savouring my drink I studied the address that was scribbled on the tissue, I knew its location, it was well within walking distance.

I made my way from the bar across the market square, through an archway into a cobbled stone courtyard to a charming mews cottage. It was colour-washed pale pink with a fine Georgian entrance door. A large 'For Sale' sign protruded from the side of the building. Pressing the door bell, there came an instant answer from the security entry phone.

'Would that be the Professor making sure that his star pupil is tucked safely up in bed?' Her voice was full of vague mischief, 'Professor' being her pet name for me during the tutorial sessions I had given her with her homework.

I answered in the affirmative. From within, the lock was automatically released.

I entered through a small hallway into an open-plan living room. The décor was contemporary yet containing many original features. It was the kind of home associated with artistic people, a bachelor girl pad. Nothing as conventional as a bedroom, but a sleeping gallery with access via a spiral staircase of fine wrought-iron work. Through the subdued lighting I took in my surroundings, the house was obviously not lived in as such, the furniture being covered by white linen dustsheets.

She appeared standing by the balustrade at the top of the stairs wearing lingerie, a shimmering transparent garment. I could see her thighs and the white lacy triangle of high-cut knickers.

'What would you have done had I not bothered to come here, phoned out for a replacement?' I jokingly asked.

Leaning over the balustrade with pursed lips she showed the tip of her tongue. 'Maybe.'

I looked about me for a suitable place I could sit without disturbing the shroud-covered furniture. On the brickwork of the raised hearth beside the open fireplace lay a large scatter cushion. I sat myself down, removing my shoes and jacket, before heading for the stairway.

The sloping roof of the sleeping gallery contained a large skylight of the kind found in an artist's studio. The bed was king-sized, being a raised pedestal in the centre of the room.

'First things first, Sally, I need to go to the bathroom to freshen up.'

The bathroom was adjacent to the sleeping area. It was large, having been fitted out to a luxury specification, complete with sunken bath, in a delicate shade of pink. I quickly freshened up, finishing off with a deodorant aerosol before putting on a white fluffy bathrobe.

She was lying crosswise on the bed, her long platinum hair hung down to the floor. Gazing up at me she giggled.

'My needs are simple; I wish to be shagged by the Professor in the moonlight. The pissed and brazen hussy that I am.' She was on a ridiculous theatrical 'passed caring' wavelength.

'Let me show you.'

Reaching towards the headboard she pulled a tasselled cord, which hung from the ceiling, releasing the blind across the large window. A shaft of moonlight fell upon the bed.

'There you have it. Instant everything.'

Lying beside her I slowly eased her knickers downwards, deftly slipping a pillow beneath her bottom. Her skin was silken smooth, with a delicate aroma of an expensive bath oil. I played with the mound of her womanhood, which was as smooth as the rest of her body.

'Why the shaved pubis?' I asked.

'It needs to be like that for when I wear my high-cut bikini briefs. It was Amanda's idea. She likes me like that when we are together. It's much nicer for you to kiss me there, don't you think?'

I duly obliged, kissing her on the naval before slowly moving downwards to her pink perfectly exposed love-lips. After a single gentle kiss, I withdrew rubbing her thighs. My curiosity was more than aroused. Amanda, I knew by sight, having seen her about the town behind the wheel of an upmarket four-wheel drive vehicle, an attractive dark-haired woman.

'You and Amanda as bedmates, I don't believe it. She doesn't come across as being at all butch.'

'Not butch Benjamin, AC/DC. Amanda likes the best of both worlds. She is very nice and gentle, sometimes men have to take a backseat.'

I was more than intrigued by her sudden, matter-of-fact revelation of such intimacies, wondering what satisfaction there would be for a female loving a female. Their physical togetherness would be somewhat limited.

'I see, tonight you wanted the real thing. There again, won't Amanda be just a teeny weeny bit jealous of me being with you tonight?'

'No, not at all, you're my one-night stand, a novelty fuck. Anyway, with you I'm in safe hands. Look at you now, teasing me to bits.'

During our pillow talk I had gently caressed her thighs, her breasts, fingering her lightly. There was a glazed far-away look in her eyes.

'I know it's been a long time, but you were the first, you were always good at keeping me waiting.'

I kissed her love-lips, she sighed her contentment, moving her arms downwards, her fingers caressing my hair and neck. As I licked her generously within, she moaned loudly, begging me to continue. It seemed an age before she came, a salty moistness on my lips.

'That's so beautiful, and now I can have you. Something better than a piece of plastic buzzing about inside me.'

Straightening up I manoeuvred her into a kneeling position on the edge of the bed, picking up a pink fluffy bedroom slipper from the floor, I gently played it about her hung breasts, along her tummy and about her ribs. As she wriggled and squirmed, I tickled the cleft of her bottom.

'You're a bitch on heat. No, I'll rephrase that, you're a pedigree bitch on heat. You need servicing, a good old fashioned dogging.'

Bending her elbows she lowered her head, leaving her rump well up beautifully displayed. The sole of her bedroom slipper was a hard shiny material. I administered three sharp slaps on each of the cheeks of her perfectly positioned buttocks. Each slap brought forth a muffled gasp. I held her by the waist rocking her bottom back and forth in a perfect penetration, tickling her ribs as she wriggled from side to side in a frenzy. I climaxed holding her to me. At the same time I palmed the white stickiness about her tummy and anointing her breasts about her pert nipples.

I awoke early, listening to the sounds of the morning from the outside world. Asleep she looked a picture of contentment, a mass of platinum blonde hair on the pillow beside me. Easing myself from the bed, picking up my clothes, I crept quietly downstairs.

The kitchen was large, neat and clean. The cupboards held very little in the way of food. The fridge stood empty, the door ajar. I soon located a jar of instant coffee and a packet of sugar. Armed with a mug of strong black coffee I wandered aimlessly about the living room.

The mantelpiece held an array of photographs of theatrical people, obviously taken from various productions she had been involved with. Amidst the ornamental horse brasses and copperware, which festooned the red brick fireplace, there was a riding whip. Taking it down from its brass hook, I ran it slowly through my fingers. It was an expensive-looking item, the handle being bound in wine-coloured leather.

Above me came the sound of movement. She appeared on the stairway, bleary-eyed, wearing a black silk housecoat with a wide sash loosely tied about her waist.

'Christ! I'm a mess, what's going on Benjamin?'

Her gaze took in my stance, standing as I was in front of the fireplace flexing the riding whip in both hands.

'I see, it's just as well you did not lay your hands on this last night.' She stood close running her index finger along the full length of the whip. 'This, I think, belonged to Amanda. She kept horses at one time.'

Amidst the theatrical memorabilia on the mantelpiece there was a photograph of Amanda immaculate in her riding outfit. She was beside her horse in a semi-bent position adjusting the animal's girth strap. It was hardly a flattering pose. Picking up the photograph I handed it to her.

'Yes, from what I've seen of her she does have a fine horse riding bottom.'

Fingering the gilt frame she studied it for some time.

'I took this at the meet of the local hunt. I don't think she likes it much which is probably why she gave it back to me.'

'Coffee?' I queried.

She shook her head. 'Not at the moment.'

The previous night's function had been a formal affair, a dinner dance organised by the local Chamber of Trade, a money raising charity event. We had sat at a shared table surrounded by lots of chatter with little opportunity for a personal tête-à-tête. In bed, the night had been one of unbridled carnal activity before drifting into a deep sleep.

'Tell me something, Sally, what happened to the last man in your life?'

She turned away waving her hand in a sweeping motion. 'He was responsible for all of this, our love nest.'

'Really?'

'He was an interior designer and quite talented, the trouble was it cost twice as much as he had estimated. Now he lives in Florida with a blowsy American creature twice his age.'

Her outburst was one of sardonic indifference.

I had a mental picture of an impecunious fresh-faced youth, straight out of some college or other, going on an extravagant ego trip.

As she reached to replace the photo I undid the sash of her housecoat so that it fell open, holding her scantily-clad body to me. With the handle of the whip hooked around my wrist, I caressed the contours of her bottom, smoothing the shiny thin fabric.

'What's this, no knickers?'

'They're there somewhere, there's not a lot of them, and you're hard.'

I gently palmed her breasts. 'And so are your nipples. We could go back to bed.'

'No Benjamin. I made a pig of myself with you last night.'

I lit a cigarette, taking a puff before handing it to her to do likewise.

'Getting back to Amanda, where does she live?'

'She lives at Orchard End House. It's an old farmhouse out on the back road, the other side of the bypass. It's a lovely place. Her husband has spent a small fortune on renovations. It has everything, swimming pool, sauna, the lot.'

'He must be a wealthy man. What's his line of business?'

'He's a senior civil servant, and fairly high up at that. During the week he stays in town, and returns home at the weekend.'

'I see. Does he know about you and Amanda? I mean... you know, being bedmates?'

Shaking her head, she giggled. 'No, he does not. He's quite happy knowing that she's not alone at night in a rather large house. There again, he is fifteen years older than her. Before you say anything, yes, she married him for security.'

'You mean money? Cosy...'

She drew on her cigarette. 'Anyway, what are you doing with yourself these days? No, don't tell me, you're a teacher at some college, surrounded by leggy female students.'

I smiled inwardly at her assessment of my present

status. Taking my business card from the top pocket of my jacket I handed it to her. She studied the ivory white card with its copperplate script.

Her response was somewhat gushing. 'My word! Antiquarian books no less.'

'Yes, that's boring old me, delving into shelves of dusty books. Nothing as glamorous as your lifestyle.'

'Not at the moment, Benjamin. I'm resting, or in plain bloody English, unemployed. Anyway, how long are you back for? Is it a weekend visit?'

'Not really. I'm busy sorting through a library of books at a large country house, way out in the sticks. The owner had decided to sell up and eventually the contents of the house will be sold at auction. It's very much the sign of the times, I'm afraid. The recession is affecting both rich and poor alike.'

She drew slowly on her cigarette. 'You can say that again, I've had my cottage up for sale for nearly a year now.'

'Where are you moving to?'

'I shall probably take a flat in town. My agent seems to think I will be better off being on the spot, so to speak, as regards attending auditions and getting noticed.'

'Let's hope he's right. I wish you well. And now I must make tracks.'

Glancing at my watch I drained the lukewarm contents of the mug, placing it on the mantelpiece. Turning to face her, I wrapped the housecoat around her body before tying the sash about her waist.

'I hope your one night stand came up to expectations.'

She stubbed the cigarette out into a large brass ashtray that stood on the raised brickwork of the hearth. 'Have you anything planned for this evening? Tonight is Jazz Night at the Old Maltings. Amanda, her husband and I are going.

It's our usual Friday night meeting place for early evening drinkies. How about making up a foursome? If I remember, jazz was your scene back in the old days.'

Inwardly I felt somewhat flattered by her interest. During my school days I had been a bit of a jazz enthusiast, playing in a knock-about quartet.

'It sounds promising, no doubt Amanda will be in her husband's bed, and you will be offering me some more of your home town hospitality.'

The conversation was interrupted by the shrill bleeping sound of the telephone, which was located in the sleeping gallery.

'That has to be Amanda, no-one else knows I'm here.'

'Shall I answer it for you?'

'No way, I'd better see to it.'

Taking her hand I looped the riding whip onto her wrist. 'In that case I'd better disappear.'

***

The remainder of the day was spent in a dusty once lived-in house several miles away sifting through a large collection of books for special rare items of literature to be catalogued. It had been a tedious operation. By the time I got back to my room at the hotel in the early evening I was more than ready for a bath and a meal. There followed a convivial hour of drinking beer in the hotel bar before heading out for the evening.

The Riverside Maltings was the town's upmarket nightspot, the ancient building having been converted to a restaurant-cum-winebar. The bar was a raised area overlooking the river, with the dance floor alongside. It was an atmospheric place of entertainment.

The bar was comfortably full. Taking in my

surroundings there did not appear to be any sign of Sally.

A group of people who had stood close by decided to leave and, through the plate glass window, seated in relaxed conversation on the terrace I caught sight of Sally and Amanda. I decided to stay put, eventually she would be bound to see me. I ordered another drink engaging the barmaid in small talk. Within a short space of time my presence had been noticed.

She made her way slowly towards the entrance doors delightfully dressed in a multi-coloured wrap-around skirt and a top in a soft printed pattern, which left her midriff exposed, bronze Grecian style sandals completed the outfit. She greeted me in a theatrical manner, kissing me gently on the cheek. The barmaid to whom I had been chatting, looked on with raised eyebrows, as if to say, 'Aren't you the lucky one.'

'There you are Benjamin, I had given you up as lost. It's getting a little chilly on the terrace, so we are coming inside.'

Amanda, looking cool in a trouser suit outfit, introduced herself, at the same time making profuse apologies for her husband's absence. He had been delayed in town. Sally, somewhat nervously, immediately took charge of the proceedings.

'Let's all sit down for drinkies,' she cooed. They made their way to a table as I set about organising the liquid refreshment. Within a minute Sally had followed me on the pretext of helping, surreptitiously whispering in my ear that on no account should I drop any hints during the course of the evening that I knew of her relationship with Amanda.

We raised our glasses, 'cheers' was said in unison. Amanda produced a packet of cigarettes, lighting up with an expensive gold lighter.

'Sally tells me you spent your school days here Benjamin.'

I nodded my head in agreement. 'That's right. I'm living and working in London at the moment.'

'Do you have a little woman tucked away in your London house? Sally's dying to know.'

Amanda's out of the blue question brought an instant response from Sally.

'Don't be so bloody forward, I said no such thing.'

I inhaled deeply on my cigarette. 'I have a girlfriend, we are engaged. Fiona is abroad at the moment in Australia. She's a teacher on one of those exchange visits that get arranged between interested parties, and she'll be away for about a year.'

Amanda pursed her lips. 'Engaged, how quaint. These days people tend to get it together under the same roof without the preliminaries. I've heard of couples needing space from time to time, but Australia, I ask you!'

Her remarks were made with an aloof bitchiness. It was an obvious reaction to my involvement with Sally.

'Take no notice, she's just a teeny-weeny bit piddled,' Sally stated. Under the table she held my hand squeezing it gently. A gesture for me not to lose my cool.

I felt somewhat peeved, I wasn't in the mood to listen to the affected mannerisms of a semi-inebriated female.

Amanda excused herself from the table. I immediately rounded on Sally.

'For Christ's sake Sally, I can do without this silly intrigue between you and her. I just can't fathom out where you are coming from. Last night you dropped your frock for me. Tell me something; is this the latest theatrical fad? A few months ago having a toy boy in tow was all the rage, now I suppose sharing your bed with another woman is the 'in' thing.'

She held her glass in a delicate pose. 'It's nothing, don't get so uppity.'

From her handbag she produced her house key, placing it on the table in front of me.

'I thought you were spoken for this evening,' nodding my head in the direction of Amanda who was engaged in deep conversation with a group of people close by.

Slowly she shook her head. 'Amanda and I are meeting her husband off the train in an hour or so, she's not in a fit state to drive, I shall take them home, and then…'

The band had started on another session, normal conversation was out of the question. She indicated that we should move to the bar away from the band. I ordered another drink, Sally perching herself on a bar stool beside me.

From then on the evening became fraught with interruptions. In the eyes of the locals, having appeared in a couple of television plays, she held a certain claim to fame. There appeared a never-ending cliqué of her friends stopping by to chat. She making the informal introductions, occasionally taking to the floor to dance. Her dancing was way-out, an exhibition of her prowess, flaunting, almost flirting, amidst a gathering of brash, trendy young men.

The band was playing a busking style of New Orleans jazz, the sound reverberating into the high vaulted ceiling of the ancient building. I was content to sit and drink, taking in the atmosphere. Eventually the evening's get together petered out. I was alone amidst the remnants of the alcoholic refreshment when Amanda came by.

'How's it with you, Benjamin?' Unlike her bitchiness earlier in the evening, her question was one of sincerity, softly spoken.

'Where has Sally disappeared to?' I asked.

'Hopefully sorting out our transport home.' She eased herself onto the stool beside me. 'Before I disappear, tell me, will you be attending the wake the week after next?'

'Wake?' I queried.

'Darling Sally's house-leaving party, a wake. She's leaving the cottage, seems the bank has pulled the shutters down on her, poor love, foreclosure on the mortgage.'

Without further ado she left. I lit a cigarette inhaling deeply, wondering why Amanda had volunteered the information of Sally's acute financial difficulties. It wasn't as if she was being malicious, almost the opposite. Swallowing my drink in one, I left, once again making my way to the cottage.

The various estate agents' advertisement boards that had once festooned the front of the business, that now stood against the garden wall, told their own story, it was very much a distress sale.

The evening's intake of alcohol had left me somewhat jaded, the shower produced a flow of lukewarm water, this, followed by a mug of black coffee, brought me back to near normality. Wrapped in a fluffy white bathrobe I lay on the king-sized bed. The bed linen held a delicate aroma of lavender. I was in a state of semi-sleep when she appeared at the top of the stairs.

Making her way to the dressing table she sat on a low stool facing me, lighting a cigarette, inhaling deeply, studying my prone outstretched body.

'Well, Professor, what was it you promised me this morning? Oh yes, a full service.'

She placed her cigarette on the rim of an ashtray, unbuttoning her top, easing it from her shoulders. Her lacy white bra was strapless, wired for maximum uplift. Her cleavage deep, the cones of her nipples rampant. Her posture was unfeminine; she sat with her legs apart, slowly unbuttoning the front of her midi-length skirt until it fell away, revealing her high-cut briefs.

'I've had lots of delicious foreplay from darling Amanda, now you can finish me with a straight fucking.'

Teasingly in a half asleep manner I answered her, 'I've had far too much to drink this evening, I'm probably suffering from a temporary bout of brewer's droop, you've come home to a reluctant stallion.'

Stubbing her cigarette out in the ashtray she sat on the side of the bed, undoing the sash of my bathrobe, gently caressing my penis. 'Tut-tut, what a disappointment.'

Lowering her knickers to her ankles she stepped out of them, at the same time unfastening her bra, so that the strapless item fell to the floor.

Taking up the dominant position, she straddled me, gently lowering her loins guiding my penis within her for a perfect insertion. Arching slowly, she rocked to and fro, lowering herself to me licking my nipples. Her long platinum tresses tickling my face, before once again propping herself onto her elbows. Slowly she rode me, her hips rotating around my erection. I played incessantly with her hung breasts nuzzling, kissing, sucking her pert nipples.

From beneath the pillow, I produced the riding crop I had secreted there earlier in the evening, placing it horizontally across my chest. Lowering her head she took it in her mouth shaking it from side to side before allowing it to fall to the floor.

'No way Professor, that's for use before, not during, and never afterwards.'

Once again she guided my throbbing tool within her, riding me in a steady rhythm. Within a short time I climaxed, she withdrew as the warm torrent flooded from me. Gasping and sighing together she lay upon my inert body.

Disengaging herself from me she took the whip to the dressing table placing it in the top drawer amidst her finest lingerie. Donning her housecoat she headed for the bathroom.

I lit a cigarette. Within a few minutes she had returned, taking the cigarette from me, and putting it to her lips.

Returning to the dressing table she proceeded to brush her hair.

'That was short and sweet,' I stated, 'compared with last night's performance, hardly a full service, for you, that is.'

She remained silent, turning her head at different angles, studying herself in the dressing table mirror.

'How much Sally? How much is owing?'

'I'm not on the bloody game, Ogilvie.' The use of the surname told of her annoyance. 'You spoil everything; you're horrible.'

'You can tell me to mind my own business if you like. How much do you owe the bank? That was my question.'

'You know don't you? You know I'm in the shit over the mortgage. Who told you?'

'A little bird, that's who.'

'Which little bird would that be, Benjamin?'

'Amanda happened to mention your house leaving party.'

'Oh, really? It's not that important, I expect half the town must know. That's the reason I moved out. One way or another I was getting pissed off with the parade of people looking over the place. Half of them were bloody time wasters.' Her clear, dulcet voice carried heavy cynicism. 'So I've left it to the estate agents to show people around. That's why I am staying with Amanda and her husband for the time being. What does a girl do when she's heading for bankruptcy? Right now I'm coming to bed to sleep.'

***

In the morning she slept as a child would sleep, a picture of contentment.

Having made myself presentable I headed back to the hotel, the young assistant manager, who was busy organising the cleaning staff in the reception area, smiled quizzically at my sudden appearance.

'I have a little celebration going on elsewhere,' I stated. 'Could you let me have the ingredients for a Buck's Fizz breakfast; a bottle of champagne, some orange juice and, if possible, ice cubes packed in a suitable container?'

'Leave it with me, sir,' was his more than obliging reply. Within five minutes he had returned with the items neatly packed in an insulated container complete with a carrying handle. Gratefully I slipped a £10 note into his hand.

Back at the cottage all was as I had left it. Having located some glasses and a large jug, I carefully mixed the drinks together adding the ice. The radio brought forth tolerable, middle of the road music.

Holding a glass of the drink, I made my way through the house. From the large open-plan living area a door led to the dining room. At the far end of the room a pair of traditional style French windows led to a small courtyard garden, containing tubs of flowers and hanging baskets. Beside the French windows, folded to its minimal size, stood a drop-leaf dining table and two chairs.

Sitting at the table my curiosity was going into

overdrive. Her way-out lovemaking appeared to be one of promiscuous desperation, a kind of wild release before she was forced to leave her home.

I wondered why the immediate members of her family had not come to her rescue. They appeared to be fairly affluent. During our school days, whilst helping her with her homework, I had been a regular visitor to her home, a lovely old red brick house on the outskirts of the town close by the river, a former mill-house with a delightful garden.

I was in the process of replenishing my glass when she appeared at the doorway.

'Don't tell me you've been out to the shops already.'

'No, not quite. What we have here is a celebration breakfast, champagne and orange juice, to bring you back to the world of the living.'

I handed her the tumbler of sparkling orange liquid. She savoured it slowly.

'It's nice, what are we celebrating?'

'Last night and the night before of course. Every actress loves praise for a fine performance.'

'Charming, that's all a girl needs to hear first thing in the morning. Are you going to give me a star rating, or just marks out of ten?'

'Actually, there is another reason. There is a way out of your present financial predicament. How would you like to be my Girl Friday?'

'I see, leave all this behind and head for some desert island with you?'

'No, Girl Friday, as in the situations vacant column of the local paper, a girl of many talents, pandering to the needs of her boss, with an added bonus, Friday night would be play night. I'm seriously thinking of taking a six month sabbatical.'

She wrinkled her face thoughtfully.

'Sabbatical, isn't that a holiday of sorts?'

'Not really, it means taking time out from what one does for a living, to pursue other interests. I was thinking of renting a cottage. It'll be nice to have a live-in housekeeper. Now that would give me an interest...'

She took my glass, helping herself to the contents, sipping it slowly.

'I think it is a little late in the day, I'm up to my neck in debt.' Handing me the empty glass she looked at me thoughtfully. 'Tell you what, I'll go and run my bath. Fetch me up a large glass of this gorgeous concoction and we can talk.'

In the bathroom she was adding some bath oil to the water, creating a mass of bubbles.

'Now for your question, Benjamin. How much... how much... how much?' Delicately, with her index finger on the steamed up surface of the bathroom mirror she wrote a large pound sign, followed by a number fifteen and the letter 'K'. 'There you have it, fifteen thou.'

Slipping out of her satin housecoat, she stood naked before me, reaching her arms above her head and gathering her long platinum hair into a stylish bob, at the same time turning her body in a pirouette movement. Her breasts and bottom were superb.

'Well Professor, can you afford me? Would I be a good investment?'

Testing the temperature of the water with her toes, she eased herself into the sunken bath.

I lit a cigarette, 'You certainly don't do things by half, it's quite a lot of money.'

'This is nice Benjamin, hand me my drink. Go into the bedroom and fetch my handbag. It should be on the dressing table.'

I carried out her instructions, returning with a cumbersome black leather bag. 'This weighs a ton, what have you got in here?'

'That's a woman's secret. All you have to do is unzip the side pocket, take out the large envelope and cast your expert eye over its contents.'

Leaning against the washbasin I studied the various letters and bank statements. It did not take long for me to digest the contents; the mortgage with the bank was some £10,000 in arrears. Her overdraft stood at £5,000, plus numerous, unpaid statements from a host of credit card companies.

'As I was saying earlier, Benjamin, it's a little late in the day. My solicitor says that unless I can put up a substantial amount of money the bank will seek possession of the cottage.'

I took a hurried puff on my cigarette, 'It's obviously a problem you can't put off, or even tinker with. I'm more than surprised they let it get this far. Have you asked your parents if they can help you?'

It was some time before she answered. 'No, Benjamin, they can't. This recession has made paupers of us all. Father's business got into serious financial difficulty. He had a stroke and was very ill for some time. They now live in a rented house.'

She eased herself into a sitting position in the bath, reaching for a towel and drying her hands. 'May I have a puff of your cigarette? I promise not to make it soggy.'

Taking a cigarette from the packet I lit it before handing it to her. 'So, they have lost their home. I'm really sorry to hear that Sally. It must have been quite an upheaval for them.'

'No, it wasn't sold. It was Amanda's husband who saved the day. He knew about an American company that was setting up a new business in the locality and they were looking for a house for one of their senior executives. They took it on a seven-year lease, putting a substantial amount of money up-front. Take the cigarette from me Benjamin, my hands are wet.'

Taking the cigarette I stubbed it out in the washbasin.

'Who knows, one day they may be able to return there. Unfortunately, it doesn't help you out of your present predicament. I'm not making any promises, but I may be able to help you.'

She looked at me wide-eyed, 'Really, tell me more?'

'I'm going downstairs for another drink. Finish your bath, no need to hurry, I shan't run away. Oh, yes, one other thing.' Repeating her earlier performance I scrawled a large £10 on the steamed-up mirror followed by the letter, 'K'.

Sitting at the dining room table I wrote out a cheque for £10,000, placing it in the top pocket of my jacket.

'Well, here I am again.' She was wearing a baggy pair of trousers and a soft cotton blouse, her moist hair piled high, pinned on top of her head.

'You were quick in finishing your bath.'

'But, of course, I can't wait to hear what you have to say. You seemed very sure of yourself in the bathroom regarding matters. What kind of trade-off are you looking for? I assume you want to share my bed for the next six months on your sabbatical? No doubt you will want me in my gymslip for you to spank me when I am really naughty?'

'I don't remember you in a gymslip, you wore a blue serge skirt and white blouse and horrible flat, frumpy shoes.'

As she aimed a playful kick in the direction of my shins, I clasped her by the waist holding her close, caressing the contours of her bottom through the smooth, thin fabric of her baggy trousers.

Turning away she released my arms from her body, looking out of the French windows. 'God, I must do something with the garden, it's a bloody mess.'

'Never mind the garden, come and sit down.'

She sat opposite me, her elbows resting on the table, her face cupped in her hands.

Taking the cheque from my pocket I placed it in front of her.

'£10,000. It's a lot of money, Benjamin.' My name in her rounded, dulcet tones gave me a certain lift. 'At least I would be safe with you. You're not like some of those silly men with quirky obsessions who love mixing with the theatrical set. Let me have a puff of your cigarette. It's a lot of money for a Friday night frolic, Benjamin. Bondage is acceptable, but bum fucking is definitely out.'

Smiling inwardly, I took the cigarette from her lips. 'I can hardly write that in your contract of employment.'

She puckered her lips in a perfect pout showing the tip of her tongue. 'If my memory serves me correctly, I think the local branch of the bank is open on Saturday mornings. Shall I pay it in right away?'

'You can get special clearance on it if you so wish. You had better phone your solicitor on Monday morning to put him in the picture. Now, follow me, he who pays the piper calls the tune.'

She followed me into the living room. I proceeded to remove the dustsheets from the furniture, scattering them about the floor. 'You can spend the rest of the day making the place habitable. I shall be back by late afternoon.'

She beckoned me in the direction of the dining room. 'Don't rush away, not yet.'

Leaning against the table she unbuttoned my jacket,

holding me by the waist, her tongue feathering my lips before penetrating my mouth. Standing on one leg she wrapped the other one about my thighs in an all-consuming vice-like embrace. It was an embrace that left one oblivious of one's immediate surroundings.

***

Having decided that my six month stay at the cottage would be an ideal opportunity for me to catalogue my private collection of books, I arranged with a removal company to transport the packing cases containing the books, plus a few items of furniture, from my London flat to the cottage. I then loaded the remnants of my previous place of domesticity into the car.

Joining the throng of weekend traffic along the M25 there followed the inevitable delay of negotiating the Dartford Tunnel. I made fairly good time, arriving at the cottage at 7 pm. There appeared to be no sign of Sally.

Having unloaded the cabin trunk, which was fairly weighty, plus the two suitcases, I placed them in the dining room. Thumbing through the pad containing various phone numbers, I soon located Amanda's number. The reply was in the form of an answer phone. Feeling somewhat peeved, I left a terse message for Sally, stating that I would be checking out of the hotel later in the evening and suggesting that she meet me in the bar at the hotel at 9 o'clock.

At the hotel I took a shower, changing into casual evening wear. The dining room, being fairly crowded with Friday night people wining and dining, I arranged for a light meal to be sent to my room.

The hotel boasted a five-star rating, it contained an element of old world elegance. There was a small bar for residents only where, in the main, sobriety was the order of the day. I ordered a large scotch with plenty of ice and dry ginger. Through the open doorway I had a perfect view of the reception area.

She arrived wearing a pair of tight fitting, plum coloured leggings, shiny, calf-hugging heeled boots and a white blouse of a smooth, synthetic fabric. Her breasts were high, with plenty of cleavage.

With the natural aplomb of a hooker, she made her way across the well-carpeted foyer towards me. She was a yard or so away from where I was sitting when she spoke.

'Hi, Professor. I understand you phoned earlier in the evening, so here I am.' It was said in a suggestive manner, as if she were some escort agency female keeping an appointment.

The young barman, busy polishing glasses on the far side of the bar, looked in my direction with raised eyebrows, as did a middle-aged couple seated nearby enjoying their after-meal coffee and liqueurs.

With a flutter of her eyelashes she eased herself onto the stool beside me. She wore her hair swept back, fastened tightly at the back of her head, and a garish amount of make-up. Compared with her sophistication of the previous weekend at the Maltings Wine Bar, where she had danced the night away surrounded by trendy young things, she was outrageously tartish.

Inwardly I knew her appearance was pure theatre.

'I do believe I've embarrassed you, Professor.'

'Not at all, it's a pity I've checked out, otherwise I could have taken you up to my room.'

She engaged in one of her favourite mannerisms, pursing her lips, showing the tip of her tongue. At the same time she glanced about her at the sedate gathering seated in the bar.

'Somehow I don't think so. There again, if the cap fits, wear it, after all, I am your captive bimbo. May I have a drink? A bottle of beer, no need for a glass.'

'Not here you don't, have a glass of wine.' I ordered the drink plus a large one for myself, indicating to her that we should retire to the terrace-cum-beer garden. The double glazed doors that led from the main bar were open. As we passed she received a wolf-whistle and a series of acknowledgements from a group of young men. We sat at a trestle table beneath a brightly coloured parasol.

'Perhaps I should parade you about the back street pubs, no doubt some big, buck Irish navvy would take a liking to you.'

'I see, you're going to pimp me about the town.' No need for that, Professor. I'm going to the ladies via the main bar. Who knows, you may have to rescue me.'

Making her way to the door she was soon engaged in what was obviously some intimate banter with her friends.

Returning to the residents' bar I replenished my glass, engaging the barman in small talk.

It was some time before she returned. 'Well, Professor, duty calls, take me home.'

It was her way of referring to our unspoken agreement. It was time to return to the cottage where she would receive some form of punishment for her somewhat contrived misdemeanours during the evening.

'Coffee? Or shall I go upstairs Benjamin?' With the use of my Christian name the tone of her voice had become servile.

'No, fix me a proper drink from the sideboard.' The luggage I had unloaded from the car that afternoon lay in disarray about the dining room floor.

'I see you really have arrived. You're not going to unpack tonight are you?'

'No, the essential items for my immediate needs I have put upstairs.' She handed me the glass of whisky and dry ginger. I took a sip and handed her the glass.

'Take it upstairs and wait for me.'

The downstairs cloakroom boasted a shower. Having freshened up I applied a liberal amount of deodorant. Within minutes, dressed in a silk dressing gown, I made my way to the bedchamber. She stood at the top of the spiral stairway, effectively barring my way. She held the cane that I had placed on her dressing table earlier in the day. Obviously, before joining me, she had not returned to the cottage, hence her sudden discovery.

Smiling, and somewhat tongue in cheek, I faced her.

'Well, I did say I had unpacked the essential items.' She held the pliant instrument with its curved handle in both hands, flexing it into a curve. Taking the cane from her I hung it on the balustrade at the top of the stairway.

She continued to bar my way. Slowly, I unbuttoned her blouse so that it hung loose about her shoulders. Caressing her breasts, palming her nipples through the thin, white fabric of her bra. Her breathing became measured.

'You're larger than usual.'

'It's that time of the month. Next weekend, for obvious reasons, I shall not be available.' Turning away, she sat at the dressing table easing her blouse from her shoulders. She proceeded to unpin her hair, shaking her head and allowing it to fall to her shoulders.

'That's enough titivating for now.' Holding the cane horizontally I gently swept the profusion of bottles and capsules containing various cosmetics to the back of the table. 'Stand up.' Tapping the cane on the stool I ordered her to kneel.

Slowly, and somewhat awkwardly, she manoeuvred

herself onto the low stool, leaning forward and placing her hands on the top of the dressing table. I switched on the fluorescent light fitting located immediately above the dressing table and at the same time switched off the centre light, leaving her undignified posture perfectly illuminated. The triple mirror gave her a perfect view of me standing immediately behind her.

'Here you are, under the spotlight, again.'

'Go easy with me Benjamin, it's been a long time.' It was an oblique reference to our after-school activities in the summerhouse of her parents' home. In the turgid heat of her adolescence she had been a more than willing partner, goading me into action. For her there had been rewards and punishments.

'It's a little late to expect leniency. As an actress you live and breath by your ego, sometimes it has to be curbed.'

In her kneeling position, her plum-coloured leggings were taut about her buttocks without a hint of a knicker line showing. The fine swell of her breasts under a spotless white bra was superb. I ran the palm of my hand over her bottom. Deftly, I unfastened her bra strap lowering it away from her body, fondling her hung breasts, holding them in the palm of my hand as if they were ripe fruit. She raised her head from its horizontal position, looking into the mirror at my reflection, wriggling her feet within her heeled boots.

'For Christ's sake get on with it.'

'What's this I hear, dissent?'

Taking the cane I laid it sharply across her bottom. Pressing her thighs tightly together, she wriggled her ankles and toes. Without raising the cane to any degree I administered a further three strokes, each brought forth a sharp intake of breath. I caressed the cheeks of her bottom.

'How is it?'

'I'm alright, finish me off.'

Slowly I continued, raising the cane higher at each stroke. The final three strokes brought forth a muted moan of pain. Her hair hung down about her face, masking her discomfort.

'Christ, Benjamin, my bum is on fire.'

I eased her leggings and knickers downwards to reveal her bare bottom.

'Well, we have the antidote here at hand, some cold-cream from the dressing table.' I selected the correct jar; gently rubbing the white substance onto her bottom, paying particular attention to the vivid pink marks the cane had left. Gently, I caressed her buttocks, lightly fingering her rose hole. She tensed the cheeks to stop me before once again releasing. She had repositioned the upper part of her body, bending her elbows and lowering her head so that it rested on her forearms.

'Benjamin, although I know we shouldn't discuss our intimacies with other people, did you ever give Fiona a spanking?'

I continued to gently massage the cold cream into her warm, tender bottom.

'Fiona was unadventurous with her sex. I spanked her once with a slipper while I was wearing my university gown and mortar board.'

She giggled, 'Is that all? Take my boots and pants off Benjamin.'

Throughout she had retained her kneeling position on the stool. I unzipped her heeled boots, putting them on the floor peeling off her leggings and knickers. She eased the upper part of her body into an upright position, running her hands through the mass of her unkempt hair. She remained kneeling on the stool.

'A perfect portrait for one of those top-shelf magazines.' I stated.

Holding her breasts, she answered me. 'My boobs are at their best this time of the month.'

She stood up rubbing her bottom. 'My legs have gone a little stiff, next time I shall put a pillow on the stool.' She stood close, kissing me lightly on the cheek, undoing the sash of my silk dressing gown, allowing it to fall open.

Taking the fluffy sheepskin rug, which lay beside the bed, she repositioned it at the top of the stairway so that it hung over the edge onto the topmost tread. 'Over here, Professor, on the stairs.'

I stood on the second step down facing her. All of a sudden she had taken control of our activities. She lay back on the sheepskin rug, her bottom positioned on the edge of the stairs, her legs wide apart, her feet resting on the topmost step of the staircase, her arms outstretched above her head, her slender fingers caressing the soft wool pile of the sheepskin rug.

Taking the silk cord from my dressing gown I gently tied her wrists together. Kneeling before her I sucked the cones of her nipples before puckering a pathway of kisses to the mound of her womanhood.

Before long she was issuing further instructions, begging me to mount her. Without further foreplay I duly obliged. Somehow she had slipped her wrists from the cord that held them. In the throes of her orgasm she grappled me to her. Her fine fingernails clawed wildly at my back. The crying of her orgasm was unreal, still she held me to her.

'Come on, come on, please, please... please...' she begged for me to climax within her. Finally, we made it together. Reaching for my dressing gown I covered our bodies. Inert we lay huddled on the floor.

Some time later she left my side, sitting at the foot of the bed sipping the whisky and dry ginger I had failed to consume earlier in the evening.

I eased myself into a sitting position, searching for a packet of cigarettes and a lighter in the pocket of my dressing gown.

Over the rim of the glass she gazed at me. 'Take a look at your back in the mirror.'

I joined her in front of the dressing table mirror, examining the vivid red slashes she had inflicted. They did not hurt me to any extent but she had certainly marked me so as to have drawn blood.

'You cruel, vicious creature.'

She giggled, 'Poetic justice, that's what.'

Taking the glass of whisky from her, I swallowed the contents. 'Should Amanda call today, I shall make a point of wandering about the house stripped to the waist.'

'I wouldn't put it past you, don't you dare!'

***

As I awoke, she lay beside me, her head resting on her arm, looking down at me, running her fine, manicured hands over my chest and squeezing my nipples.

She spoke, 'You don't have a hairy chest, that's nice.'

I murmured a reply, 'I'm glad you approve.'

'Your name doesn't suit you. Benjamin is a biblical name for a gentle, kind person. You're a sadist, you beat Sallykins.'

For a moment she exuded the child/woman image of our long ago summer, when, in her newfound womanhood, she had interrogated me with a sweet naivety on the ways of love as we lay side by side on the wicker sun bed in the summerhouse.

'I'm not a sadist, you're a masochist. I pander to your needs. One could say you bring out the worst side of my nature.'

'You have an answer to everything you, don't you?'

Leaving the bed she stood before the dressing table, adjusting the mirror, turning sideways and examining the cheeks of her bottom, rubbing them in a circular motion.

'My poor bot, it's feeling tender.'

Putting on her housecoat, tying the sash tightly about her waist she stood at the foot of the bed, hands on her hips, in a dominant posture.

'Let's try something different. Lie on your tummy.'

I duly obliged. She eased the duvet to the foot of the bed leaving my back and bottom fully exposed. She had taken the cane from the dressing table. In an awkward manner she raised it striking me lightly on the buttocks.

I laughed. 'You will have to do better than that.' The second stroke carried a little more force. 'Getting better.' I quipped. The third stroke really stung. 'Bitch!' I shouted, twisting sideways.

'Keep still,' she commanded, 'there's more to come.'

The following stroke was but a mere slap. She tossed the cane to the floor. 'No, definitely not for me.'

Rubbing my bottom she replaced the duvet about my naked body.

'I see, the status quo remains.' My remark went unanswered. She lay on the bed, her housecoat wrapped about her body, gazing up at the ceiling. Gently rubbing the smooth fabric of her hands about her tummy, opening the garment, fingering her pubis.

Kneeling beside her I undid the sash of her housecoat, revealing her naked body. At the same time she had taken the pillow, easing it under her bottom. Taking the sash of her housecoat I gently, but firmly, tied her wrists together, fastening them to the headboard. She remained silent.

Leaving her wrists tethered to the headboard I replaced the housecoat about her body.

From the bathroom I could hear moans of defiance as she struggled to free herself. Sometime later she appeared naked at the bathroom door.

'I was coming back to deal with you,' I bantered.

'No you were not, you were being cruel to Sally. We can do it here.'

We showered together, she claiming the plastic shower cap, the soap on a rope shared between our bodies.

***

As regards Sally, everything was on a high. Her life-style could continue as one of the beautiful people about town with a mews cottage dwelling, a GTi car and the continued use of her credit cards.

Since my arrival the dining room had been converted into a study-cum-den. A massive desk with a fine leather top took pride of place in the centre of the room. Along the far wall floor to ceiling shelving had been installed in readiness to house my collection of books. There was also a Victorian chaise longue, a place to read and relax, and to make love in the afternoons.

My collection of books was not over large, but selective. The task of cataloguing them could have been achieved by any self-respecting librarian within a few days. With Sally as my assistant it was an informal arrangement to be enjoyed with lots of chat.

During our mid-morning coffee break we sat amid a clutter of packing cases, the floor littered with books. She was wearing a shirt and a pair of cropped leggings that came just below her knee in a black satin-smooth fabric.

She sat on a packing case, her elbows resting on her knees, her face cupped in her hands, reading a book that was resting on her lap. Beside her, with its hinged lid open, was the cabin trunk.

'I found your hoard of naughty books, Benjamin.'

'Really, what's that, Lady Chatterley's Lover?'

'No, silly, I read that yonks ago, when I was at school. Come to think of it, you lent it to me.'

'I see, you've raided my treasure chest. What classical literature have you graduated to then?'

She held up a small volume in a black leather covering, the title being embossed in gold leaf.

'Oh, De Sade, no less. Perhaps you should keep that for some bedtime reading.'

'No way. It's hardly a turn on for any girl. Some poor bitch has been taken to a glade in the forest, stripped naked and tied to a tree. The man then lays into her with a carriage whip. It's horrendous!'

Somewhat tongue in cheek I answered her, 'Are you saying that kind of activity should only be carried out behind closed doors?'

She raised the book in her hand as if to throw it at me.

'Don't do that, it's worth a lot of money, it's a very early edition.' I eased myself into a semi-reclining position on the chaise longue. 'In some respects you are probably right. De Sade was somewhat barbaric. Domination of the fair sex requires a certain finesse. If you look at the flyleaf on the book, someone has scribbled a French proverb: "He who chastises most, loves most." Submission is a female trait, how far to take it, that is the question, all part of the agony and the ecstasy of masochism. There again the incidence of male masochism to female masochism is probably equal. One only has to pick up a copy of a tabloid newspaper to read about some company director, or senior executive, who has the power to hire and fire people at will, taking himself off to some back-street brothel for a dose of degradation at the hands of some well-built Madam.'

'You're very knowledgeable about kinky pastimes, Professor.'

'It's human nature. The latent deviant desires of many a man or woman.'

'The book that was doing the rounds amongst the girls at drama school was, 'The Story of O'. I read a couple of chapters before passing it on. Being chained to a bed all night long is not my idea of togetherness. No doubt you have a copy?'

'No, I don't. It's a fairly contemporary publication. I have read some of it, the message in the book is of a woman deeply in love, submitting herself to the ultimate in degradation.'

My comments went unanswered. She was selecting another book, turning the pages at random as if to find an interesting chapter. She continued to read the book, obviously engrossed in its contents, at the same time slowly rotating her stockinged foot on the deep-pile carpeting.

'Well, have you found yourself a good read?'

She puckered her lips in an impish grin.

'It's not bad; it's a novel of sorts, set in Victorian England at a large country house. One of the servant girls, having been given the afternoon off to visit the local town has arrived home very late, the housekeeper, an ugly old cow, has decided she has to be punished so, with the help of a footman she has been put across the kitchen table, her skirts lifted, her drawers lowered to her ankles and given a few strokes of the birch, the footman holding her down as she struggles and screams. The poor bitch then scuttles off to her bedroom. Reading on a bit further, the footman turns out to be the girl's secret lover, so within a short time he's also in her bedroom. You can guess the rest.'

I drew on my cigarette, 'Those kinds of goings-on were commonplace in the homes of the gentry; even erring wives or daughters could be dealt with in a similar fashion. Until the Rights of Women Act was passed by Parliament in 1870 women were owned by men.'

Putting the book to one side she stood up, walking towards me, 'I know what you're thinking; it was a good job I wasn't around then.'

She knelt on the floor beside me. 'May I have a puff on your cigarette?'

I handed her the packet, 'Help yourself.'

She lit a cigarette, inhaling deeply.

'I forgot to tell you; Amanda phoned yesterday evening. She was up in town attending some function or other with her husband. She would like me to go over to Orchard End this afternoon.'

Amanda's visits to London to be with her husband were frequent. Men in his position needed the appendage of an attractive wife. Having a wife many years his junior was obviously an asset.

'I absolutely forbid it there's far too much work to be done here. Look at the state of the place; books all over the floor.'

She immediately saw through my pedantic refusal. Unbuttoning a single button of my shirt she slid her hand onto my tummy, gently caressing my naval, moving her hand downwards, attempting to ease her fingers below my belt.

In one swift movement I placed my hands on top of hers, trapping them.

'Time and place for everything.'

I eased myself into a sitting position. 'I don't quite understand, Amanda's up in town but she wishes you to go out to Orchard End.'

She drew on her cigarette, holding it away from her in a delicate pose.

'She has an ulterior motive. Some months ago they had a break-in, she was obviously hoping to be back there by this afternoon. In the mornings they have a part-time gardener. It's just a case of having someone about the place to keep an eye on things.'

'I see, Sally's Security Service. Say there were intruders, how safe would you be?'

'No problem, they have an arrangement with the gardener, his Alsatian dog is kennelled in one of the outhouses, and I have my mobile phone.'

'Fetch me another cup of coffee and I will think about it.'

Within a few minutes she had returned with the coffee.

'Anyway, why don't you come over with me?'

Armed with my cup of coffee I headed for the desk, sitting down on the high-backed chair, swivelling it to face the French windows, gazing out into the sunlit courtyard garden.

'I'm sorely tempted at that.'

She perched herself in a half-sitting position on the edge of the desk beside me, swinging her leg to and fro.

'You really are a dull dog, Professor, we can swim and then retire to the sauna or a nice bubbly spa bath.'

Taking my cup of coffee, she placed it on the desk, leaning forward, nibbling my earlobe, whispering, 'I know what you will go for. Sauna equals Swedish massage equals you know what.'

***

Orchard End House, a timber-framed farmhouse lay about two miles out of the town. Beyond a wide sweep of gravelled driveway there was a huge barn building of red brick and tarred weatherboard. The swimming pool being located at the far end of the barn building, well screened from the roadway. A section of the building adjacent to the pool had been tastefully converted into a pool house. It contained changing rooms and a mini gymnasium with a selection of multi-exercise equipment. The sauna was a small cabin clad in pinewood.

Sally, in true Beverly Hills' style and dressed in a bikini, was lying on a sun bed beside the pool. She acknowledged my arrival with a wave of her hand.

'Gorgeous, isn't it?'

I made my way to the far end of the pool slowly taking off my lightweight slacks, shirt, socks and shoes to reveal a brightly coloured pair of boxer shorts.

'Very sexy,' she shouted.

'I don't possess any bathing trunks.'

Having swum a couple of lengths I emerged beside her; she threw me a towel.

'Don't you dare splash me.'

Beside her in a small insulated container there was a bottle of wine and glasses plus the book she had borrowed from my collection. Shaking open a deck chair, I sat beside her.

'Is it a good read?'

'I'm only reading tiny bits, some of it is a little heavy for me.'

Taking the wine bottle from its container I studied the label, it was half full. 'Drinking too much and swimming isn't good for you, Sally.'

'I've had my dip; I'm sun bathing now. A little later I shall take a cold shower and then it will be time for a sauna bath. What more could one ask for? It's like attending a health clinic. Pour yourself a drink, it's my favourite sparkling white wine, nice and bubbly.'

Lying back in the deck chair I savoured my drink.

Donning a pair of outsized sunglasses and adjusting her sun bed to a fully reclining position, she lay back.

From the side of the pool there was a perfect view of the back of the house. 'The house is much larger than it appears from the road,' I stated, 'more than enough room for two people.'

'They tend to do a lot of entertaining; people visiting at weekends.'

Her reply was one of indifference; she appeared reluctant to make conversation. Her bubbly enthusiasm earlier in the morning, regarding spending the afternoon together, was no longer evident.

Finishing my drink I stood up, taking one pace forward before leaping into the pool, the cascade of water showering her outstretched body. As I dog-paddled my way to the far side of the pool she shouted after me.

'You bastard!'

'Sorry, it was an accident,' I countered.

Lethargically I swam a length of the pool. Having towelled herself she headed off in the direction of the pool house swaying her hips in an exaggerated manner, looking back at me over her shoulder. Within a few minutes I had followed her, stripping off my boxer shorts and leaving them to dry in the sun. Having showered and draped in a towel, I headed for the sauna cabin, gingerly opening the door a few inches and peering inside. She was lying flat out on a narrow slatted pine bench with a towel covering the lower part of her body.

'I must be mad letting you in here. Make sure the door is bolted, sometimes the gardener comes back in the afternoons.'

Several bundles of birch rods were stored in a stone jar in the corner of the cabin. I picked one up.

'Now here's something different, something you can't buy at Harrods.' Half turning she adjusted the towel about her middle.

'I cut them from the wood last time I was here. They have been in soak ever since to soften them. Most of them that is! Well it's your highlight of the afternoon Benjamin; go easy. Amanda's very good at it; before she got married she was a beauty therapist.'

'Fondling of other female bodies must have appealed to her,' I bantered.

'Sometimes you're bloody unkind,' she retorted.

Her sudden defence of Amanda had been unduly sharp. Since my arrival at Orchard End she had appeared a little subdued, somewhat on edge.

The birch twigs rustled gently in the air as I applied them across her back and shoulders turning her skin a gentle pink. The session of massage continued for some time. She remained immobile, her head resting on her folded arms. As I slid the towel away to bare her bottom, she turned to face me.

'I suppose from now on I'm going to get the full treatment?' Straightening her arms she gripped the edge of the pine bench, tensing her body.

I drew the birch twigs lightly across the backs of her thighs.

'Ogilvie, you're a bloody tease; just do it.'

With a little more aggression I applied the birch across her bottom. At each stroke she shouted defiance, 'Pig! Bastard! Prat!' eventually begging me to stop, 'That's enough, my bottom feels like it's been stung by a swarm of wasps.'

Slowly she stood up rubbing her bottom vigorously before wrapping a towel about her body. 'I'm going to put some clothes on.' She kissed me lightly upon the lips. 'I'm sorry Benjamin.' Somehow I knew exactly what she meant. It was all to do with territory. The cottage was our love nest. Here at Orchard End, somehow it did not quite work out.

This was confirmed when she said, 'Amanda called on her mobile phone, she is coming back earlier than planned. Her husband is catching a later train.'

I got dressed holding up my sodden underpants for her to see.

'I shall have to travel home without my undies.'

***

It was about 9.30 p.m. in the evening when she returned to the cottage. Preparing a light supper of salad, we ate in the kitchen.

'The clothes I wish you to wear are laid out on the bed ready,' I stated in a sombre tone of voice, 'and then come down to the study.'

Taking the bar stool from the kitchen I carried it through, placing it immediately in front of the desk. Within a short time she had joined me, dressed in her black satin housecoat. Her underwear was minimal; she was braless, her white briefs were of the high cut variety, with black, self-supporting stockings and scarlet shoes with spiked heels.

Placing a velvet cushion on the stool I indicated to her to sit. With perfect deportment she did so, her legs crossed. Her housecoat hung open revealing her wide cleavage.

Taking the book she had been reading during the day, I handed it to her, 'Now then, read me one of your favourite chapters.'

Moving to the far side of the desk, I sat down on the swivel chair immediately opposite her. In her clear, dulcet tones, mimicking the various voices of the characters, she read me a chapter, about a wayward female who defies her father's wishes by associating with a local ne'er-do-well. Returning on horseback her father confronts her in the stable, ordering the groom to hold her while he lays into her with a riding crop. The groom, a sadistic man with a permanent leer about his face, enjoys the spectacle immensely. During the recital she had crossed and uncrossed her legs in a delicate pose.

I rose from my chair. 'Very good, I enjoyed it.'

From the study doorway I watched as she negotiated the spiral stairway in the ridiculously high-heeled shoes, it was poetry in motion.

The night had become humid, hot and oppressive. Opening the French windows I looked out into the night sky. Far beyond the town a flicker of lightening lit the sky followed by a distant roll of thunder. Somewhere a storm was brewing. Leaving the door ajar I drew the curtains and dimmed the lights. Having activated the CD player I lay on the chaise longue with a large glass of whisky and dry ginger amid the drifting sound of classical music.

A short time later she came into the room without speaking fixed herself a drink.

Slowly she made her way towards me, allowing her housecoat to fall from her shoulders. She was dressed, as earlier in the evening, wearing a minimal amount of underwear.

'Here comes your expensive plaything, Professor.'

She knelt beside me, sipping her drink, her free hand

slid beneath my dressing gown gently fingering my penis. 'What's this, still without undies?'

Putting aside her drink she undid the dressing gown, sliding her hand under the small of my back to manoeuvre me towards the edge of the chaise longue.

'Come this way, lie flat so that I can get at you.'

I eased my body into a horizontal position. Gently she tongued and licked my erection, slowly her pursed, sensual lips held it within her mouth, holding and sucking it for some time before withdrawing.

'God, you're tense. I'll give it to you straight.'

Slowly she mounted, rocking to and fro about my erection. 'Now then Professor, without the whip I shall ride you far into the night.'

***

The following morning I was busy sorting through a mountain of mail when she put in an appearance.

'Where have you been this early in the morning, Sally?'

'I took the car to the garage for a service. It hasn't been done for yonks.'

'Unlike its owner,' I quipped.

Within a few moments she had realised the significance of what I had said, giving me one of her theatrical pouts and wrinkling her nose.

She was wearing a pair of tight fitting trousers in blue linen, with an oversized white shirt that hung below her waistline, held by a wide leather belt with a snaffle buckle.

'Did you go dressed like that?'

'But of course, the lads down at the garage workshop were most appreciative, they promised that they would have the car ready by this afternoon.'

'As my assistant librarian you should dress accordingly. A mid-length skirt, blouse and some sensible shoes.'

She perched herself on the edge of the desk. 'Bullshit, Benjamin, bullshit. You know you wouldn't have me any other way. You can ogle my bum to your heart's content. Now then, what do you want me to do?'

'At this very moment, not a lot.' I indicated the pile of packing cases that were stacked against the far wall of the study. 'Providing I can locate my hoard of packaging materials I shall parcel up a few books to be despatched to one of my valued customers. They need to be sent by registered post, so I shall have to make a trip to the post office. This afternoon I shall have to pay a visit to the second-hand furniture shop out on the main road. Apparently, over the weekend they carried out a house clearance. As well as furniture there were lots of books, so they want me to give them the once over. There may be one or two valuable items there.

'So, that's my itinerary for the day. The next thing is to get you organised. I suggest you get on with some of your housework for the next hour or so.'

Leaning across the desk she kissed me lightly on the forehead. 'I love it when you try to be bossy. You're not very good at it, except at bedtime of course. I shall go out and do some shopping and by the time I get back it will be coffee break.'

By mid-morning she had returned. In the meantime I had been organising things in the study. The drop-leaf dining table had been opened to its full size and covered with a green baize cloth. The computer terminal being set up on one end of the table.

'Perfect timing, I'm just about ready for you.'

'Really, that sounds ominous. Shall I make some

coffee?'

'No. Wait until I come back from the post office. In the meantime I have a special treat for you. You can carry on from where you left off yesterday, unpacking the cabin trunk.

'Let me explain to you how the system will work, hopefully, that is. As you unpack the books, place them on the tabletop and then later on I shall enter them on the computer. Once they have been entered on the computer they will be put on the shelves and then they will be put back into the packing cases. This time round the packing cases will be clearly marked with the contents. In other words, the shelving is but a temporary holding area. It's simplicity itself. Oh, yes, one other thing, just unpack the books from the trunk. There are lots of other goodies in there; I shall have to find another home for them.'

She puckered her lips, 'Understood, Professor.'

'I shall leave you to it then.'

On my return I was in the kitchen preparing coffee when she appeared at the doorway.

'Surprise, surprise, Professor. I wouldn't have taken you for one of the punk people.'

As she spoke she raised her arms into the air. On both her wrists she wore leather, metal studded bracelets.

'You're a naughty girl, I told you to unpack the books and leave the other items. Go on through, I'll bring the coffee.'

Placing the tray with the coffee mugs on an upturned packing case, I sat on the chaise longue. She had taken up her favourite position, squatting on the floor beside me. Leaning forward I dragged the cabin trunk close to where we were sitting.

'It's not as you say, punk fashion, but some serious items of bondage. We may as well finish unpacking it. At the same time you can have a full dress rehearsal.'

'No way, Professor, I know what's in there, whips and things. Where on earth did you get all this stuff?'

'I'm not one of the dirty mackintosh brigade who frequent back-street porno shops. The man who put this collection together had good taste; all of it's beautifully made. You won't find any handcuffs, they are for criminals, and the whips are lightweight. The collection was obviously used for the punishment of the fair sex.'

I savoured my coffee, glancing about me. 'Can you fetch me my cigarettes from the kitchen? I'm sure that's where I've left them.'

Having lit a cigarette I settled back on the chaise longue. 'Now then, I will tell you how I acquired the cabin trunk and its contents.

'One day I kept an appointment at a fairly large house, way out in the middle of nowhere. The owner had died and the contents of the house were being prepared to be sold off. I had finished carrying out an inventory of a fairly large bookcase and was about to leave when the woman took me to an outhouse to where the cabin trunk was stored. It had obviously been taken out there on purpose because she was acutely embarrassed about its contents and on no account did she want them to be included in the sale, so I made an offer to purchase them there and then. There you have it. As a matter of fact the previous owner was in your line of business, something to do with the theatre. What it was exactly, I never did find out.

'Tell me something, were you offered any work in blue movies at all after you left drama school? You know what they say, the word 'actress' covers a multitude of sins.'

She looked at me quizzically. 'No, never. Mind you I did know one or two girls who were really hard up who did do that kind of work. It was usually carried out in some makeshift studio or other. One of them then got a decent part in a long-running television soap. Some tabloid newspaper reporter dug up the fact that she had been involved in blue movies. Well, it's just not on, is it? I'm not into porn.'

I stubbed out my cigarette. 'I'm not talking about porn, I'm talking about pale blue movies, there's a big difference. With pale blue movies we are talking eroticism, deviant physical love, way out foreplay which enhances love making.'

Replacing the coffee cup on the tray I sat on the edge of the chaise longue.

'As I was saying, the cabin trunk contains the private life of a man who was associated in some way with the theatre.'

From a deep pocket that was located within the lining of the cabin trunk I withdrew a small folder. 'Take a look at this – film scripts of you know what.'

Placing the sheaf of neatly bound papers on her lap she studied them intently, reading each one in turn before placing them on the floor beside her.

Gathering up the tray and the empty coffee mugs I made my way to the kitchen.

Returning to the study I lit a cigarette, taking a puff before handing it to her. 'Well, what do you think? Speaking as a non-thespian, they're nothing more than a series of three sketches of erotic cameo items, wouldn't you say?'

Inhaling on her cigarette, she nodded. 'They were obviously played out in private, one man, two women. No doubt they were written by the man, each of the females being humiliated in turn. Extremely voyeuristic, he takes great pleasure in ordering one female to be chastised by the other for some minor misdemeanour. Unfortunately Professor, you only have little ol' me.'

Uncertain of her reaction to what I was about to propose, I lay back on the chaise longue, gazing up at the ceiling.

'How about Amanda, for a cameo roll alongside yourself?'

'What! Absolutely no way! Christ, you're serious aren't you?'

'You could have the lead role,' I stated in a light-hearted manner.

Leaning across my prone body she held my wrists as if to wrestle with me, at the same time placing her lips on mine in an all-consuming kiss.

The conversation was interrupted by the sound of the doorbell. Hurriedly she stood up, at the same time removing the metal studded bracelets from her wrists.

'Christ, that will be Amanda. She said she was going to call round for coffee.'

I gave a hollow laugh, 'Perfect timing, talk of the devil. Invite her in so we can chat.'

Tossing the bracelets into the cabin trunk she closed the lid. 'No way, I shall take her through to the kitchen with the excuse that you are far too busy to be disturbed.'

***

Returning home Sally's car was parked on the forecourt, immediately in front of the house. A young man wearing blue overalls stood nearby. As I parked the Mercedes he eyed me keenly before speaking. 'I brought the young lady's car back Sir, I don't think she's in; I've rung the bell several times.'

In his hand he held a buff envelope, 'The boss told me

that I should pick up the cheque.'

Closing the car door I took it from him opening it, it was a bill for some £150. Leaning on the car bonnet I wrote out the cheque handing it to him. 'How are you getting back to the garage? Shall I give you a lift?'

'No, thank you Sir, I've finished for the day.'

Taking some money from my pocket I gave him five pounds, 'Here you are, have a pint on me.'

In the kitchen, preparing a cup of tea, I came across the note she had left. It was short and sweet, stating that as a working girl she had decided to go for an after-work drink along with some of her friends.

***

The saloon bar of the White Hart Hotel was the early evening drinking venue for the local office workers on their homeward journey.

Their entrance would be at orderly intervals, in the main. The company was masculine with a smattering of females looking suitably decorative. All in all it was very much a clique scenario.

They had their own unwritten rules. Mobile phones and shop talk were strictly taboo. Beyond their brash sophistication they were somewhat an effete bunch. Amidst this gathering, perched on a bar stool, she was obviously in her element, she was wearing a pencil-slim skirt and seamed stockings, spiked-heeled shoes and a well-cut blouse with shaped silver buttons. Her skirt being split at the front, was fastened by umpteen buttons, being partially unbuttoned, no doubt viewed from the right distance and angle a certain amount of stocking top and a glimmer of white thigh would be visible. She was chic, but suggestive. The outfit she wore was obviously directed at my comments earlier in the morning, regarding her mode of dress.

She acknowledged my arrival with a coquettish wave of moving fingertips. I raised my hand to indicate that I would be in the other bar.

I was in the process of ordering a drink when she joined me.

'Ogilvie, you're being bloody anti-social.'

'No, not at all. I was waiting for you to join me as I have something for you.'

I handed her the envelope containing the bill from the garage.

'Oh God, more expense. I didn't expect it to be that amount.'

'It's not a problem, it's been paid.'

'I have a feeling it's going to cost me.'

'In your own words you wouldn't want it any other way. Drink?'

'No, I have one in the other bar.'

Picking up my glass I immediately followed her.

The group of people with whom she was ensconced I knew vaguely, having met them at the Maltings Wine Bar the previous week. They greeted me warmly. I hovered on the fringe of the company, joining them in their mild, ineffectual bar-room banter. From what I could gather Sally had consumed more than an adequate amount and was flirting unashamedly in a bubbly, effervescent manner.

Gradually the evening's get together came to an end. One by one various members took their leave, heading homewards to their wives or mistresses.

Suddenly she held my hand squeezing it tightly, whispering in my ear, 'Take me home Benjamin.'

***

She stood framed in the study doorway, leaning against the doorpost, her handbag dangling from her hand, the nonchalant pose of a street girl.

I had taken up my favourite position, lying in a semi-reclining position on the chaise longue.

Slowly she entered the room placing her handbag on the desk, she stood a few yards from me.

'Now Benjamin, what has been on display all evening in the bar is yours.'

Removing her blouse slowly she held it at arm's length before allowing it to fall to the floor, unfastening her skirt, she eased it downwards revealing her black suspender belt and knickers.

Slowly she made her way to where I lay, kneeling on the floor beside me.

My response was immediate, 'Come on, let's do it.'

Wrinkling her nose she teasingly shook her head, slowly from side to side.

In one slow movement I slid from the chaise longue to the floor beside her grasping her by the waist, kneeling astride her body, holding her to the floor.

'What's this, dissent from a lazy girl who spends half the day swanning about the town?'

Retaining my position, from the cabin trunk I produced the leather-studded bracelets that were fastened together by a short length of silver chain. Deftly I fastened them about her wrists. Her struggles to avoid this were feeble, but a token gesture. As I removed my lower garments she lay there, inert.

Slowly I rode her. All too soon her arms encompassed my body, clutching me to her, her hands partially clenched, her fine fingernails gouging my back.

We lay for some time, the carpet soiled beneath our bodies. She wriggled her bottom, 'Sex is such a messy business,' she murmured.

Slowly together we stood up, the straps of her suspender belt and her stocking tops smeared with semen.

***

From the open doorway she watched me as I took a whip from the open cabin trunk. It was a short handled instrument with six knotted thongs of finest leather.

With the handle looped around my wrist I lit a cigarette, slowly pacing the floor before her.

Momentarily she held me to her before slowly making her way up the spiral stairway to the bathroom.

For an age she commandeered the bathroom before appearing wrapped in an oversized pink bathrobe, her hair swathed in a towel, commenting that the night was young, it was only nine o'clock, and she felt peckish, therefore I should send out for something to eat.

Half an hour later carrying a tray containing her favourite pizza of cheese and pineapple and lots of salad, I made my way up the spiral stairway.

She was sitting cross-legged on the bed gently towelling her hair dry. Scattered on the bed beside her were of the cameo film scripts taken from the trunk.

'What's this, getting ready for rehearsals?'

'No way. What you put me through this afternoon is here somewhere.'

Leaning back on the headboard, she placed the plate of food I had provided for her on her lap.

'Aren't you going to eat?'

'No, I'm going to have a shower.'

I showered in a leisurely fashion, allowing her time to

finish her meal.

By the time I had returned she had taken herself off to the kitchen, busying herself in the domestic chore of washing-up.

When she returned I was sitting on the stool beside the dressing table, holding the whip and leather bracelets

'Don't you dare think about it, Benjamin.'

'Now that I've allocated them to your wardrobe I shall treat them accordingly with some of your expensive perfume.'

'No you don't. Use that ghastly musk muck, that should go well on leather.'

Taking it from me she held it up, at the same time spraying it liberally from an aerosol of inexpensive perfume. Looking me straight in the eye she slowly wrapped the thongs of the whip about its handle before placing it in the top-most drawer of the dressing table.

'Out of sight, out of mind, Professor.'

Laying crossways on the bed, running my hand over the duvet cover I indicated to her to join me. Slowly she did so, unfastening her bathrobe revealing her naked body. Having attended to my dressing gown likewise, she mounted me.

Fresh-faced, devoid of make up I held her freshly-washed body to me. She rode me for some time; still within her we changed positions, allowing me to dominate. Slowly, methodically, I carried on the operation as she held me to her, lightly fingering my neck. Her orgasm was some time in the making, sighing her fulfilment, her legs about me.

***

The following week became a time of simple pleasure,

sorting books being of secondary importance, the evenings being spent wining and dining, doing the rounds of the various bars about the town.

Occasionally she would head out on her own, indicating to me the places she would be visiting, I would then leave her to her own devices. When in conversation with a male admirer in some crowded back street bar she would look at me from a distance holding a bottle of beer in one hand, she would caress her thigh and bottom with the other in a blatant show of body language.

On one occasion when returning to my side she stated, 'This isn't any good you know; here I am pandering to the locals for the benefit of your ego. I'm rapidly getting a reputation for being a tease. One day I shall stay out all night and then you will be jealous.'

Her ultra-feminine mood of attitude continued about the cottage. Each and every time we made love it was at her bidding. Be it on the chaise longue in the study or in the bedroom, and of course on the floor at the top of the spiral stairway, lying upon a sheepskin rug occasionally indulging herself in some self-imposed bondage by fastening her wrists with the leather metal studded bracelets within a multi-orgasm. Her finely manicured fingers clasping the chain which held her. Gently releasing her wrists from their bondage, I had carried her bodily to the bed placing the duvet about her naked body.

One Sunday evening as I lay on the chaise longue in semi-sleep she kissed me lightly on the forehead announcing she was off to Orchard End House and Amanda. It was to be a girls' night together.

It was mid-morning before she reappeared entering the study from the French windows. She wore a summer frock in a delicate flower print, the waistline gathered below her bust, a shapeless yet fashionable garment, her legs slender and tanned. Perfectly manicured toenails protruding from her open-toed sandals.

Sensing her sombre mood I attempted a little humour.

'Where are you off to this morning? Is it coffee at the vicarage?'

'Definitely not, I'm off to see the bank manager. He wishes to see me. Apparently he wants a statement of my financial affairs.'

'Financial affairs, that sounds ominous.' My reply was one of mock seriousness.

She stood at the desk beside me peering over my shoulder, reaching out my hand I gently fondled the contours of her bottom swivelling my chair, putting my hands around her waist, guiding her to sit on my lap.

Amidst the letters I had received that morning there was a pale blue envelope embossed with an airmail logo. A letter from Fiona in Australia. The letter had been redirected to me from my London address.

'I suppose it's silly of me to ask, I assume Fiona doesn't know about me, like you've taken yourself a mistress?'

'No, I told her I was going to rent a cottage out in the country for six months and that my mail would be forwarded on to me. In the words of a diplomat, I was being "economical with the truth". Anyway, we have an extremely adult relationship; no doubt she will be doing her own thing. Let me introduce you.'

Reaching into the bottom of the drawer of the desk I produced a framed photograph of Fiona. Taking it from me she studied it intently. It was the kind of photograph that any proud parent would display on their sideboard, a portrait of a pretty young woman in an academic gown complete with a tasselled mortarboard, a photo that had been taken at a university graduation ceremony.

A hint of a smile crossed her face. 'She's very pretty.' She handed back the photo, which I duly replaced in the desk drawer.

'The thing is, Benjamin, what shall I say to the bank manager?'

'I can't answer that it all depends on what he has to say to you. You could tell him that the £10,000 cheque I gave to you was for a collection of books that I'd purchased. A family heirloom, so to speak. There again, with my car being parked on the forecourt, morning, noon and night, I expect it's common knowledge I'm shacking up here.

'Anyway, bank managers aren't that interested in where the money comes from, as long as they get their hands on it. I've just thought of something else, perhaps you should declare it to the Inland Revenue as earnings.'

During our conversation she had remained sitting on my lap, pinching my thigh immediately above the knee, which in turn sent me wriggling and squirming. She posed the question, 'Meaning?'

'As my housekeeper of course. For myself I don't think a mistress is tax deductible.'

Standing up and leaning forward she whispered in my ear, 'Ogilvie, you're a pig. Just be here when I get back.'

She left via the French windows. I followed her progress until she had disappeared through the doorway of the walled garden.

Having fixed myself a cup of coffee I, too, wandered about the tiny courtyard garden, which even to my untrained eye looked a picture.

I wondered why she hadn't mentioned her appointment with the bank manager previously. Reflecting on her mood swings during the past week on our forays about the town on what was a glorified pub-crawl, she had exuded the image of a wild child. It was very much a repetition of her behaviour when she had first seduced me back into her life. Then, as now, it was financial pressure that appeared to trigger off her way-out behaviour.

***

Anticipating her return I had placed the chair in the centre of the room. Tossing her handbag onto the chaise longue, she headed for the sideboard.

'The man's a shit of the first order.' Without adding to the statement, picking up the ice bucket she flounced from the room returning within minutes attacking its contents with an ice pick before adding some ice to her gin and tonic.

In her clear, dulcet tones the crude invective continued. 'A little shit of a man. Would you believe it, having paid off the mortgage arrears the little toad wouldn't extend my overdraft.'

Since her return and the following outburst I had sat, nonplussed.

'I thought you were on fairly good terms with the bank manager?'

No, it wasn't him, he's away on leave somewhere, it was the young assistant manager, a fresh-faced little twit. I needed the overdraft to pay off my credit cards.'

I swivelled my chair in a complete circle before answering her. 'Doesn't really make sense Sally, you are borrowing from Peter to pay Paul.'

She lay back on the chaise longue gazing up at the ceiling. 'Please don't lecture me Professor, I've had enough for one morning. He also suggested that I should drop the price on the cottage, the property market being what it is. Anyway, he's going to review the situation in about three months.'

'Bully for him,' I quipped. I got up wandering about the room. 'Well, I have the perfect remedy for you; let me take you shopping.'

Taking the partially filled glass from her I placed it on the sideboard. 'It's far too early to be hitting the hard stuff.'

For her our shopping expedition was an extravaganza of indulgence. She just loved nice things. On the way back she insisted on taking lunch at a quiet pub close by the river.

Over lunch she had become a little preoccupied. 'A penny for your thoughts?' I asked, pouring the last of the white wine into the tall-stemmed goblets.

'I was thinking about what that wretched man said at the bank this morning. Without appearing ungrateful, Benjamin, perhaps I should have moved out and let them take the damned place.'

I savoured my wine. 'You're way off the mark there. The bank would have probably sold the house at auction at some ridiculously low price; you could have ended up still owing them money. There's no point in brooding about it, time is on your side. When you go back to see them in three months things could very well be different. Finish your drink and I will pay the bill.'

On our way back to the car we made a detour to the far side of the river. Suddenly with childlike abandonment, her arms outstretched, she ran on ahead of me into a plantation of weeping willow trees. I followed in a mock manner of pursuit; finally we came to rest in a hollow on a grassy bank, engulfed in each other's arms.

For some time we lay side-by-side, our arms wrapped about each other. The dappled sunlight filtering through the fronds of a Weeping Willow tree fell upon our inert bodies.

Suddenly she wriggled free from my grasp. 'Let me up

Benjamin, the ground's damp. I think I'm sitting on a molehill. Christ! Look at the state of my dress.'

She stood up brushing away fragments of dead grass from her skirt, twisting sideways examining the mud stain on her posterior. 'Let's go, Benjamin.' Stretching out her arm she helped me to my feet.

We drove slowly back to the cottage. She sat beside me in a semi-reclining position. Her frock unbuttoned, showing a gorgeous amount of her legs. Driving one-handed I caressed her thighs; placing her hand on my searching fingertips she remained passive to my advances.

Back at the cottage she made a hurried dash for the kitchen, kicking her shoes aside, at the same time unbuttoning her frock, allowing it to fall to the floor. In one movement she eased her tights and knickers down to her ankles, stepping from them.

As she bent forward to place the garments in the washing machine I held her by the waist brushing my arousal against her. Kicking and struggling she attempted to escape, her feminine modesty denying me.

'You're a bloody animal, Ogilvie.' As her wriggling and struggling subsided I manoeuvred her towards the tall stool that stood beside the breakfast bar. Without further resistance she bent over it. The upper part of her body resting on the work surface.

The cumbersome handbag, which stood nearby, fell sideways, partially spilling out its contents.

Amidst the clutter of cosmetic capsules lay a plastic, transparent container containing a long slender dildo. It bore a foreign label and logo, which left very little to the imagination regarding its use.

'Well, well, well, what do we have here?' I exclaimed. 'How embarrassing, say you had an accident and some stranger had to look into your handbag for identification.

What on earth would they think?'

'It's an old handbag for keeping odds and ends, I don't use it as such, Benjamin. It's usually over at Amanda's.'

'That I can see, looking at its contents.'

Picking up the offending instrument I eased it from its container, fingering its slender sheath. As sex aids went, it was delicate, exquisite.

'This is anal. I didn't think that was your scene. At least that's what you told me, remember?'

It was some time before she answered, her reply being barely audible. 'It's Amanda's, she likes it.'

Gently rubbing the cheeks of her bare bottom I held the dildo aloft, 'And this?'

'I tease her occasionally with it, Benjamin, and she did me once. I don't think I could describe it, I nearly exploded, half crazy.'

Ordering her to remain where she was I drew the curtains across the window.

Like on many previous occasions she had retained the crude carnal position passively, the upper part of her body resting upon the breakfast bar. Occasionally clenching the cheeks of her bottom and her thighs together, before once again relaxing them.

She glanced at me from her ungainly position. Reaching out she deftly picked up a large towel from the laundry basket easing it beneath her, adding, 'My tits are cold.' As she took up her previous position I gave her bottom a sharp slap.

Rummaging amidst the various cosmetics and lotions I selected a bottle of baby lotion, gently fingering the rose of her bottom I applied a liberal amount. She remained passive gripping the far side of the breakfast bar slowly rotating her bottom. Gently I eased the dildo within her. With her face buried in the towel there came a sharp intake of breath, splaying her legs she gave a deep sigh. Guiding the dildo to and fro her sighing became a gurgling crescendo, her bottom twisting and wriggling, her acceptance of pleasure couched in the voice of rejection.

'Oh, God, no... no... no more please.'

Gently I withdrew the slender sheath from within her quivering bottom.

Wrapped in the towel she stood on tiptoe puckering my face with numerous kisses.

'You've just touched every nerve end in my body, I've been in another world.'

***

Amanda was a frequent visitor to the cottage, engaging Sally in their own brand of girl talk. On these occasions I would discretely disappear.

One afternoon the auction I had attended having very little to interest me in the way of books, I returned home earlier than planned.

On my arrival back at the cottage I could hear giggling and chatter coming from the sleeping gallery. Amanda and Sally were on the bed together. Amanda being dressed, Sally being topless wearing her skintight black Lycra leggings and calf hugging heeled boots. The modern gadgetry they used for their pleasures lay on the bedside table.

As Sally disappeared in the direction of the bathroom I headed back down the stairway to the study. Within a few minutes I had been followed. From the open doorway I surveyed the scene.

Amanda had taken it upon herself to have a drink. She stood at the far side of the room beside the drinks cabinet. I immediately joined her pouring myself a whisky.

'Well, I think a few words are in order? What do you have to say for yourself?' I lit a cigarette, savouring it to the full. From the beginning of our cohabitation Sally had insisted that I should not divulge to Amanda that I knew of their relationship. Having witnessed their intimacies that afternoon, the situation was mine to exploit in any way I chose. She had perched herself on the arm of the settee, at the same time rummaging through the contents of her handbag for her cigarette lighter.

'Perhaps we should adjourn to the study?' I stated. Through pursed lips she exhaled a perfect ring of smoke in my direction.

'No thanks, I can guess what happens in there, you're the prat with the laid-back libido who likes to lay on a bit of stick before performing.'

'Mandy and Sallykins, birds of a feather that sleep together,' I bantered. 'Surely your husband shafts you occasionally? After all he's home most weekends.'

'That's none of your business. Don't be so bloody crude.'

'Perhaps I should phone him at his London office,' I replied, 'with a singular request, "kindly keep your wife out of my mistress's bed".'

'You can please yourself about that, somehow I don't think he would be that bothered by your tittle-tattle.'

Beneath her bravado I could sense a certain nervousness.

'Personally, Amanda, I'm not bothered either. Had I been into kinky threesomes I would have jumped into bed with you both. You and Sally together are acceptable, there is something nice and delicate about two members of the gentle sex laying each other.'

Once again she exhaled a perfect smoke ring from her cigarette. 'I am not staying here to listen to you.' She stood up. Naturally enough from the very outset she had shown defiance.

'Sit down, I haven't finished with you yet.' The tone of my voice brought an instant response. Slowly she eased herself onto the arm of the chair.

'In this part of the world sophistication is a little thin on the ground, wouldn't you say. Should the coven of bitches who congregate at the aptly named Rumours Tea Shop find out about your life as a closet lesbian, can you just imagine their titillation when you happen to be about the town?'

'What are you saying, Ogilvie?'

'What am I saying, you ask? Just this; you need to appreciate the realism of the situation and exercise discretion at all times.

'With your husband away from home during the week, you have far too much time to indulge yourself. You should keep your activities within the confines of your country house home.

'Trust you to make an issue out of it. You don't really care.' Abruptly she stood up stubbing out her cigarette in the ashtray before turning to face me.

If ever a telephone had rung at an inconvenient moment, it was then. I had a second phone line located in the study, which was known only to my customers in the book trade. Quickly I dashed to answer it.

It was an American gentleman, a valued client. The transatlantic time lapse being as such, he was phoning me from his home at breakfast time, before leaving for the office, here it was mid-afternoon. It was a long and protracted conversation regarding some obscure titles he was attempting to track down.

Having dealt with the matter as quickly as possible, I returned to the sitting room. Amanda had obviously left.

From outside the door I heard the sound of Sally's car revving up. Glancing through the window I was just in time to see her drive away with Amanda in the passenger seat.

It was an hour or so later I telephoned Amanda's house. It was as I had expected, being answered by the bland tones of an answer-phone machine.

***

In the early hours of the morning I was aware of her arrival, feigning sleep I remained prone upon the bed.

Drawing aside the curtains she stood aloof, her arms folded in a questioning posture, lighting a cigarette, inhaling deeply, looking beyond the window before turning to face me.

Opening my eyes I questioned her, 'Yes, so?'

'You're a bastard, you really gave it to her didn't you?'

Obviously they had exchanged lots of chat. I eased myself into a sitting position, leaning against the headboard. 'Come over here, let me have a puff of your cigarette.'

She immediately tossed the packet of cigarettes onto the bed in front of me.

'Come over here.' The tone of my voice was one of mild authority. Slowly she made her way to the bed, sitting down beside me. Her housecoat hung loose about her shoulders. Within her lacy white bra the cones of her nipples were prominent.

Taking the cigarette from her I inhaled deeply before placing it in the ashtray on the bedside table.

Reaching out I gently caressed the contours of her breasts. 'You're at your best after sharing Amanda's bed. Come to bed with me.'

Taking my wrist she manoeuvred my hand away from her. 'Not now, Benjamin.'

In one swift movement I gripped her wrist pulling her onto the bed. Kicking and struggling she attempted to break away. We wrestled for some time before she gave in.

Throwing the duvet to the foot of the bed she sat astride my naked body. Unfastening her bra she tossed it to the floor, looking me straight in the eye, she unfastened the delicate ribbons that held her knickers at the waist, pulling them away from beneath her.

'He who pays the piper calls the tune, is that it?'

'Of course not, don't be silly, there again you carry a fairly high price tag.'

Slowly she mounted me taking the weight of her upper body on her outstretched arms, rocking slowly to and fro.

'It's all changed, it's different now. You shouldn't have involved Amanda. You should have left things as they were.'

'Like what? You strutting your stuff about the town, showing out all over the place. Me hunting you down.'

'Well, at the end of the day you got what you wanted didn't you?'

'True. What happened with Amanda was for the best; after all I respected your confidence about your relationship. Also she doesn't know that I knew about it before finding you in bed together. Now that would have been unkind. She is very protective towards you without being one of those strutting feminist creatures.'

My observations had gone unanswered. She continued to ride me in a methodical, unfeeling manner. I palmed her breasts, fingering her nipples, maintaining my prone position. I reached to the floor attempting to locate the riding whip. Realising my intentions she held my wrist shaking her head from side to side.

'Come on, Sally, sulking doesn't suit you.'

Relaxing her outstretched arms she lowered her body so that she lay beside me absent-mindedly fingering my chest. 'You're a patronising twit. From now on it's going to be strictly housekeeper duties only.'

Gathering up her underwear, she headed for the bathroom, calling out over her shoulder. 'Breakfast will be in half an hour.'

Over breakfast she remained cool and aloof as if unsure of the new situation that had arisen.

Once again I broached the subject. 'With Amanda on-board our little triangle is complete.' It was some time before she replied.

'What's this, another trade off, is that it?'

'Well, threesomes are out.'

Leaning forward across the table I took the glass of orange juice she held from her hand, placing it on the table. 'I couldn't agree more, share and share alike. As I said earlier, she's not one of those strutting feminist creatures, and she has you as her playmate in her country house home, whilst her husband is away in town. So no more secrets.'

Her reply to my appraisal was somewhat terse. 'Well, Benjamin, we shall have to see. You don't own me. I'm you're live-in housekeeper, remember?'

Following breakfast I retired to the study dealing with the mundane matter of the morning mail, pondering on the happenings of the previous twenty-four hours.

For her, the remainder of the morning was spent in domestic efficiency, the sound of the vacuum cleaner echoing throughout the house.

It was past midday when she appeared at the study door tapping lightly on it before entering. She was wearing a pair of cropped, ragged jeans, and a cheesecloth blouse. Beneath the fine fabric the outline of her black bra was clearly visible. Over her shoulder she carried a large, multi-coloured beach bag.

'Your housekeeper is now going off duty. I've left you a cheese and ham salad in the fridge for lunch. That should save you a trip to the pub.'

I levered myself out of the swivel chair. 'Hang on a minute don't disappear just yet. What about this room?' With my outstretched arm I indicated to the shelves of books and the top of the desk. 'It needs a damn good going over, after all it's the most important room in the house.'

Still with the door partially opened she hovered as if eager to get away. Her annoyance was obvious. 'You should've said something earlier on. I'm not a bloody mind reader.'

I beckoned her into the room. 'Where are you off to this afternoon, then?'

Amanda's, where else? I'm going over for a swim and some relaxation.'

I sat back down on the chair swivelling it to face the French windows. 'Who knows? I may join you later on.'

'If you do, you'd better phone Amanda.' She turned to go; her farewell was made in a tinkling high-pitched voice, 'Bye-ee.'

The tone of her voice was meant to tease. Her petulance during the morning was something contrived in a feeble attempt to punish me for my involvement with Amanda the previous afternoon. I immediately reached for the phone, dialling the number at Orchard End House. Within a few seconds Amanda's clear tones came over the line. Without any preliminaries I immediately posed the question, 'I understand you're have a pool-party this afternoon. I was thinking of popping along a little later on.'

Her reply was also immediate, 'Why not, if you must.' The tone of her voice off-hand, bordering upon rudeness.

I immediately replaced the receiver. In phoning her I had been deliberately intrusive. They were obviously looking forward to a girlie afternoon together.

Having eaten the lunch Sally had prepared for me, plus consuming a half-bottle of fine white wine, driving the car was out of the question.

Wearing a T-shirt and a pair of lightweight trousers I walked out across the fields, heading for Orchard End House, an easy trek of some one and a half miles.

Being on foot my arrival had gone unnoticed. Slowly I made my way to the far end of the barn building through an ornamental brick archway to the secluded area of the swimming pool. Stopping short I surveyed the scene before me. Sally and Amanda were stretched out completely naked side by side on their sun beds. They were laying face downwards and holding each other's hand, their fingers entwined.

Feeling slightly embarrassed I stood absorbed, an observer, a voyeur of their nakedness. Sally, blonde lithe and tanned, Amanda, curvaceous, her legs apart, her bottom inviting.

Silently I turned retracing my steps back to the gravelled driveway. Sally's car was parked nearby, the ignition key protruding from the steering column. Switching on I sounded the car horn loud and clear in a long intermittent burst. Lighting a cigarette I hovered beside the car for a minute or so before once again retracing my steps to the swimming pool.

They had vacated their sun beds and were standing at the far end of the pool. On my appearance I received a fleeting wave of a hand from Amanda, then naked, hand in hand they leapt into the water. They swam a length of the pool together, their free hands propelling them along. As they reached the end of the pool where I stood they turned, their bare bottoms clearing the water as if in some erotic synchronised swimming movement.

Their display was strictly for my benefit. Together they were on a high, they were females with attitude flaunting their sexuality.

On leaving the water their modesty had returned, immediately wrapping their bodies in outsized bath towels.

Together in animated conversation they walked beyond the immediate area of the swimming pool. Sally's eye contact with me was unresponsive; at the same time a hint of a smile feathered her lips. I was obviously still out of favour.

Within a minute, clutching the towel about her, Amanda headed back in my direction.

'Well, Benjamin, you decided to come. How did you get here?'

My reply was terse. 'On foot. It's Sally I came to see.'

She adjusted the towel, hitching it up to ensure her breasts were fully covered. 'She's gone into the house to change before popping out to the shops for me. I'm sorry about this morning, on the phone that is. You caught me on the hop so to speak. I'd only just put down the receiver after speaking to my husband phoning from town. He's coming home this evening. Anyway, aren't you going in for a dip?'

I shook my head. 'I don't have a costume.'

She giggled. 'When in Rome, do as the Romans.'

I reached out my hand as if to ease the towel away from her body. 'Are you coming in as well then?'

She shook her head. 'No, I'm off to have a shower.'

Once again, tongue in cheek I went on the offensive. 'I see, your husband phones you, and I get the sharp end of your tongue.'

Turning away I aimlessly wandered along the edge of the swimming pool before once again returning to her side. 'I've just had a long hot walk here, perhaps I should join you in the shower?'

Gazing over my shoulder she looked towards the house. 'No, Benjamin, time and place for everything.'

I stood close to her, resting my hands on her bare shoulders. 'Well then you can exercise some of your other talents by giving me a massage.'

'Righto. Mind you, strictly therapeutic, nothing more. I shall take a shower and while I'm making myself presentable you can shower.'

Following our encounter the previous afternoon, her unquestioning acceptance surprised me. As she made her way to the shower room I called after her. 'Not too presentable.'

The massage table stood adjacent to the sauna cabin and the changing room. Amanda appeared wearing a baggy pair of lightweight trousers and a black bra top. With a towel draped about my lower regions I positioned myself flat out, face downwards. She proceeded to massage my back in a vigorous, business-like manner.

'Gently, gently.' I bantered.

'You're not flabby or fat, just pale and flaccid; this will do you a world of good. Anyway, you don't have too long, Sally's only gone down to the shops, and she's popping into the cottage to fetch something to wear for this evening. Perhaps you should have been there, Benjamin.'

'Really. Tell me, what's happening, your husband coming home and Sally getting into her glad-rags?'

'As I was saying, my husband is coming home this evening. He's bringing a guest for an evening meal. A lone male, probably a member of some overseas trade delegation or other. I'd like Sally to make up a foursome.'

'Well, what can I say Amanda; she shared my bed for but an hour earlier this morning. Once again I'm playing second fiddle.'

Moving to the top end of the massage couch she gently manipulated the flesh between my shoulders and neck. 'Sometimes it can be difficult keeping a husband happy. He can be a very demanding person.'

She obviously valued the security of her marriage, financial and otherwise. Her ready acceptance of a session of massage was fairly obvious, she needed to talk. This was borne out when she said, 'Anyway, Sally says you're looking for an arrangement between us. What kind of arrangement, Benjamin?' As she spoke she had moved to the bottom of the massage table, easing the towel from my bottom, sliding it down so that it lay draped about my feet and ankles.

'We all need our sexual playthings, Amanda. Three makes for a more exciting encounter, don't you think?'

Using her hands in a chopping motion she lightly pummelled the backs of my thighs. The flesh moving involuntarily under a steady rhythm. She remained silent for some time, raising my head I looked beyond the pool room window towards a small plantation of ancient apple trees and a neat, railed paddock.

'What are you thinking of now?' she queried.

'I'm thinking about the wonders of living in the country behind closed doors, that is.'

She produced a bottle of oil-like substance, delicately rubbing it into my shoulders and about my upper torso. It gave off a pungent, yet not unpleasant, smell. 'What's that you're using?'

'I don't know really, I'm not an aromatherapy person. It's masculine I can assure you, probably something like sandalwood.'

With a circular motion of her hands she continued to massage my back before wiping her hands thoroughly on the towel. Gently she smoothed the cheeks of my buttocks.

'I'd better not do your bot.'

'Why not? It's nice, it's doing things to me down below.' Slowly I rolled over onto my back, at the same time easing my body towards the bottom edge of the couch.

'Come down a little further,' she ordered. Rubbing my thighs her fingers found the uprising of my penis. With the other hand she had located the lever at the side of the massage couch, a mechanical device for adjusting the height. Having lowered it sufficiently, she proceeded to remove her bra top, bending forward so that her breasts hung either side, allowing my penis into her cleavage, gently manipulating her breasts about it.

'That's beautiful. Finish me off.'

'No, Benjamin, I'm not into what you want, nothing oral.'

Obviously, that was one of her inhibitions. No doubt that particular intimacy was reserved for Sally's love-lips.

'As regards your so-called agreement, Benjamin, threesomes are smutty.'

Obviously, her objective in approaching the subject was to reject it. I, in turn, was feeling wonderfully relaxed. 'Never mind the chat, Amanda, take off your pants and climb aboard, screw me.'

As I spoke there came the sound of a car on the gravelled driveway.

In a lightening movement she replaced her bra top, at the same time placing the towel across my lower regions.

'Make yourself presentable. I'll go and give Sally a hand to unload the shopping.'

I had barely finished dressing when Sally arrived at the pool room door.

I'm helping Amanda with this evening's meal thingy. I take it she's told you? You take the car and I'll get a taxi. There again, I may stay the night.'

Her manner was cool, uncaring. As she handed me the car keys I held her hand in a positive manner. 'Be back by 11 pm or I may come over and fetch you.'

Her voice was one of mock surprise. 'My word, the Master has spoken,' followed by a cryptic note, 'we shall see.' With an exaggerated flounce she turned towards the door.

Once alone I headed for the sauna cabin. From the stone jar, which was part of the interior fittings, I selected half a dozen birch rods. They were freshly cut, being springy and supple. No doubt Sally and Amanda had intended to have a sauna bath together. Stripping the excess green foliage from the stems into a waste bin I stowed them in the boot of the car.

***

It was 11.30 pm when she returned, obviously testing the ultimatum I had given her earlier in the day, that she should return by 11 pm, to its limit.

Her entry into the house was barely audible, the door being carefully opened and closed as if to avoid any confrontation.

Opening the study door I greeted her. 'In here please. Don't try and sneak away.'

'I wasn't. I was just taking my bag upstairs.'

She was wearing a simple black dress, narrow shoulder straps that were tied at the shoulders by delicate bows.

'That's a pretty dress you're wearing. A pleasant evening was it?'

She wrinkled her nose. 'Not really, the man sitting opposite me was middle-age, fuddy duddy, full of the usual synthetic chat.'

She followed me into the study. From a considerable distance, taking deliberate aim, she threw her beach bag onto the chaise longue.

I had prepared for her return in a meticulous manner; a tall bar stool having been placed immediately in front of the desk on which lay the large black volume of nineteenth century erotic literature.

'Well, Professor, I see you couldn't bear to go to bed before your bedtime story. It must be some kind of hangover from a deprived childhood.' Her off-hand disapproval of the evening she had spent at Orchard End House was now one of flippancy, with a hint of sarcasm.

Ignoring the tone of her voice I placed the velvet cushion onto the stool and sat down. I handed her the book that was open at the appropriate page.

'I've chosen one of your favourite stories. The one you found quite exciting. It's all about a servant girl who returns to her place of employment late and is dealt with in an appropriate manner. Anyway read it to yourself as a re-cap while I indulge myself with a glass of brandy.'

Pouring myself a drink I wandered towards the French windows and drawing the curtains before returning to the desk. From the top-most drawer I produced a pair of white cotton gloves, placing them before me.

'As I was saying, a further rendition of that particular item is not required, actions speak louder than words.'

Taking the book from her I replaced it on the bookshelf. Slowly donning the gloves I faced her. 'Now we shall see how well you have performed your duties.'

Using one finger at a time I tested the bookshelves for dust, wandering about the room running my finger along the top of each and every picture frame that I could reach. Once again returning to stand immediately in front of her, holding up my hands the fingers outstretched before her, they were now a dirty grey colour, smudged with a residue of dust.

'You lazy, lazy creature, so much for your swanning off in the middle of the day, before completing your housekeeping duties.' Removing the gloves I allowed them to fall to the floor, quickly opening the top drawer of the filing cabinet that stood adjacent to the desk. From it I produced the metal studded leather wrist bracelets, each having a short length of chain attached to them. From the bottom drawer of the cabinet I removed the birch rods I had brought from Orchard End House that afternoon. They had been meticulously prepared; the thicker ends being liberally bound in red adhesive tape, so as to form a handle. A brush of twigs perfectly splayed to form a perfect instrument.

My somewhat pompous lecture on her wrongdoing was all part of the ritual of an ongoing game; an item of erotica contained in the book would be played out in a cameo of subservience and obedience.

During my lecture she had remained silent perched on the stool, fingering the hem of her skirt, smoothing the fabric about her thighs. At the same time there was a clicking of her high-heeled shoes on the foot rail of the stool as she wriggled and twisted her feet.

I held the birch rod lightly swinging it against the side of my leg in a rhythmic fashion. 'It was good of Amanda to let me have these, don't you think?'

Her response was instant. Immediately stepping away from the stool so that she stood close by the desk.

'Somehow, I don't think so. You probably sneaked them into the boot of your car.'

Picking up my partially consumed glass of brandy she swallowed it in one. Unfastening the shoulder straps of her dress from her shoulders, reaching her hand behind her back to unzip it, pulling it downwards so that it hung about her waist. The fixed stare remained as she unfastened the black, strapless bra allowing it to fall to the floor, wriggling her bottom and thighs she eased the dress to her ankles before stepping from it. She was wearing a black suspender belt and dark stockings of a fine denier and lacy knickers in red and black. Removing her knickers she held them aloft, allowing them to drift slowing onto the top of the desk. Removing it from the desk I held the brief garment in my hand, my fingers caressing the soft, moist fabric.

I handed her the leather bracelets. 'Put those on slowly.' Awkwardly she obeyed. Taking up the birch rod I stood beside her. Without further command she bent over the stool, her arms outstretched gripping the lower rail. As I fastened her wrists about the rail, she spoke in a low voice. 'Not too many, Benjamin.'

Caressing her bare bottom I unfastened the suspenders from her stocking tops, tucking them into the waistband of the suspender belt, easing her stockings downwards, fully exposing the backs of her thighs.

'Not too many, you say. That is for me to know, and you to find out. Keep a count if you can bear to, and let me know when I ask.' From her bent-over position she mumbled her compliance.

Slowly I drew the birch rod across her bottom, teasing and tickling the backs of her thighs. As she wriggled and squirmed I brought it sharply down. At each exquisite stroke she gave a sharp cry of pain.

Having paused I posed the question, 'How many?'

'That's six,' she snapped. The tone of her voice carried defiance. I laid the birch rod squarely and sharply across the back of her thighs.

'No, not there.' Her voice was now contrite.

'Yes, madam,' I replied, 'Yes, there.'

Following it with a further stroke, moaning loudly she gripped the lower rail of the stool. Her knees buckled beneath her and with a final flourish I allowed her a further stroke.

Having unfastened the chains that held her wrists I led her through the doorway into the sitting room securing her wrists to the spiral stairway immediately above her head before once again returning to the study. Pouring myself a liberal measure of brandy with a touch of dry ginger, I sipped it slowly. With the glass in my hand I wandered into the lounge switching on the wall lights. They were of a contemporary design, spotlights that could be focused in any direction so as to enhance the décor. I focused them in her direction before once again returning to the study. Fully illuminated, framed in the doorway, she presented a perfect picture of bondage. Her head hung forward, her long blonde tresses partially covering her face. From her lips came a muted request.

'Please, Benjamin, fetch some cream for my bottom. Christ, I'm sore all over.'

'All in good time,' I replied. 'All in good time.'

Taking the velvet covered cushion from the study I placed it immediately on the floor before her. Unfastening the suspender belt from about her waist and the two straps that were still attached to her stockings, slowly I knelt on the cushion before her, kissing her navel, my hands gently caressing her bruised, burning bottom. She gave a low gasp, from within her body came a tremor.

'Now I shall pay homage to my love slave,' I murmured, 'a woman who understands the pain and the pleasure of the flesh.' Slowly I kissed her love-lips, feathering my tongue within her, caressing her thighs.

Having unfastened the chain and the leather bracelets from her wrists, I handed her the glass of brandy. She sipped it slowly running her hand through her hair, pushing it into some semblance of order.

Our early morning pillow talk was an on-going ritual. She awoke early releasing the roller blind which covered the skylight window immediately above where we lay, flooding the room in sunlight. I, in turn begging her not to as I wished to lay in semi-darkness to doze.

Having granted my request she proceeded with a finger examination of my body, fingering my nipples and navel. Caressing my thighs, playing with my dormant penis in an attempt to tease me into life, goading my inactivity by whispering in my ear, 'Useless, useless tool!'

'No peace for the wicked,' I murmured.

Nibbling my earlobe she replied, 'You can say that again, wicked, wicked, wicked. I barely slept a wink.'

She was wearing one of my T-shirts, which barely covered her bottom. Once again she lay on her tummy, her head slightly raised, resting in the crook of her elbow.

'Remember back in the old days in the summerhouse, you were really pissed off with my antics, you wanted to impress Dad by making sure I got my 'A' Level grades, and I was more interested in a fuck so you spanked me with a table tennis bat. I kept the bedroom door locked when I was changing, if Mum had caught sight of my bottom, Christ knows what she'd have thought.'

I gave a hollow laugh, her masochistic reminiscence was somehow endearing.

'It's not funny.'

I manoeuvred myself into a sitting position. 'I wasn't laughing at you. Let's have a cigarette.'

Lighting a cigarette she took a puff before handing it to me. 'Marvellous, isn't it, booze, bed, a shag and a fag. Don't you agree?'

Ignoring my inane observation her thoughts were elsewhere.

'You shouldn't have done the end thing with me last night. Tying me up and kissing me all over. You should have put my bum on that leather sofa and screwed me there and then.'

'I see, I shall know next time, shan't I?' Digging her elbows into my ribs she pushed me sideways. Recovering my balance I held her by the waist. 'Now then, tell me about Amanda – let's hear all your girlie gossip. Things were fine yesterday until you came storming back from your shopping trip... petulant creature.'

'I had every reason... the day before when you came back to the cottage and we were upstairs together, you really upset her, she thought you were being serious.'

'She's capable of looking after herself I would have thought.'

'You haven't met her husband, Benjamin; he's a stuffed shirt. Christ, if he ever found out about you know what... talk about wounded masculine pride... God knows what would happen.'

'It could be worse,' I stated, 'what if she were having an affair with the gardener?'

She giggled, 'He's bloody ancient, anyway it's sorted, in Amanda's eyes your second name is discretion, with a capital D. I've made sure of that, she likes you... and,' she leant forward nibbling my earlobe, whispering, 'she may even take part in a kinky cameo play thingy with you, the one where it all happens in the stable. And now, before you get any further ideas, I'm going to get dressed.'

I lay back on the bed, which was bathed in the early morning sunlight. It was easy to visualise the embarrassment it would cause should Amanda's relationship with Sally become common knowledge.

Her husband, who spent his working day wandering the corridors of power in some Whitehall office as a senior civil servant, would no doubt be the subject of gossip of the worst variety if it became common knowledge that his wife chose to share her bed with another woman.

Dressed in tight fitting jeans and a black bra, she was in the process of putting on her make-up. We had eye contact via the triple dressing table mirror.

'What are you scheming now Benjamin? No, don't tell me... I can guess... Amanda, a promise maybe?'

'Actually, I was thinking about her husband. You could be playing a dangerous game. After all, the man has feelings... or is it a pretend marriage?'

'No, it's not a pretend marriage, it's the real thing, remember what I said, discretion is a must?'

I eased myself from the bed, slipping into a bathrobe. 'A promise you said, from Amanda, tell me how is it she came to read the cameo plays? They were meant to be kept private.'

'No, they were not. We read them together while sunbathing by the pool yesterday.'

Having finished putting on her face, she stood behind me, her head resting on my shoulder. 'Now then, let's be civilized for a change and have a proper sit down breakfast and you can talk to me lots and lots.'

***

At about 10 pm on the Sunday evening I headed down the motorway to London. The traffic was fairly heavy with returning holidaymakers from the east coast resorts. It was well after midnight when I arrived at the flat. I felt tired one way or another it had been a long day. I opted for the settee, which was one of the put-u-up variety. Taking a duvet, a sheet and a couple of pillows from the bedroom, within two minutes the bed was ready to take my tired body. I slept fitfully.

In the morning the sound of traffic along the main road told me it was quite late. Glancing at the clock on the mantelpiece the hands pointed at midday. According to my wrist watch it was 9.30 am.

I made my way to the bathroom. A bath was called for, not a shower, I wanted to soak and relax and plan for the future.

The sole reason for my flying visit back to town was to collect mail. Having failed to renew the arrangement to have letters redirected by a given date, many items of correspondence had not arrived at the cottage.

The bath water was getting cold; reaching out my foot I operated the hot water tap. Of course, there was Fiona my intended; highly organised Fiona, her future mapped out before her. Not for her a back-packing jaunt around the world before settling down to a career. She had taken herself off to Australia on an exchange visit working as a teacher, all of which had been carried out in a businesslike manner. Her London flat being let out so as to cover the mortgage payments.

Of late, Fiona's letters and phone calls had been less frequent, at the same time extolling the wonders of the Australian way of life, they often included photographs of beach barbecues and poolside parties. Reading between the lines there appeared to be a certain message within them, they contained frequent mention of a man from the Education Department who had apparently taken her under his wing as a lone female in a strange country, adding that there was a strong possibility that she would be staying on for a further three months or so. On the surface it appeared an open-ended arrangement, a vague hint that our engagement should end.

Delaying my return to the cottage so as to avoid the rush hour traffic, it was close to midnight by the time I arrived there.

She was sitting at the foot of the stairs, her hands on her knees, dressed in an ankle-length winceyette nightgown, her face devoid of any make-up. It was the kind of nightie that a schoolgirl would don before climbing into bed on a cold winter's night.

I greeted her with peck on the cheek. 'I love your baby doll nightie.'

'Baby doll nightie?' she giggled, 'this isn't a baby doll nightie. That would be a tiny top barely covering my tits with a pair of frilly knickers to match. Where have you been Benjamin. You wouldn't catch me wearing anything naff like that.'

'Oh, really?'

She gave me her standard response of wrinkling her nose.

'Anyway, I waited up especially for you. Guess what? Someone wants to buy the cottage.'

Her childlike enthusiasm had completely disarmed me. I immediately turned away heading for the study and the sideboard. 'What I need is a drink.' She followed me. 'Are you having one?'

'Just a teeny weeny one of whatever you're having.'

I handed her the drink. Perching herself on the arm of the chaise longue, she immediately burst forth with the day's happenings.

She had received a phone call from the estate agents saying that they had received an offer for the cottage. It was for £10,000 less than the asking price. Apparently the offer had come from a London agent acting on behalf of a retained client.

Swallowing my drink in one, I poured myself another. 'Are you going to accept it?'

'I phoned the bank manager late this afternoon and he seems to think that I should, the property market being what it is at the moment.'

Feeling uncomfortable I made my way to the far side of the room, opening the curtains of the French windows and looking out at the night sky before turning to face her. 'He's probably right. Anyway, let's talk about it in the morning.'

Slowly we made our way up the spiral staircase. By wearing that particular night attire she was making a statement; she wanted comfort and togetherness without sex.

During the night it rained heavily with the cold rattle of rain on the skylight above us, she snuggled close to my body. I held her gently, caressing her body through the brushed cotton fabric of her nightie.

By the morning the rain had subsided in the bright sunshine. From the bedroom window I caught sight of her in the courtyard garden. She was barefoot, wearing a faded blue summer frock. Armed with a pair of kitchen scissors she was busy cutting roses that were looking somewhat forlorn after the heavy overnight rain. In the damp dew-fresh morning she held a drifting ethereal quality.

Back in the kitchen she busied herself cutting away excess foliage before placing the flowers into a large glass vase. Once again the conversation revolved around the sale of the cottage.

'I suppose now that the cottage is going to be sold I shall be getting my marching orders? Sorry, I'm being selfish, where are you going to live? That's the important question.'

Without thinking I had blurted out an off the top of my head question which I had immediately attempted to retract.

She continued to arrange the flowers in delicate manner, absorbed in her task. 'It won't happen overnight, I shall work something out, remember I've been there before, or very nearly.'

'Now you will be able to return to London, back to theatricals,' I stated, 'After all, I still have my flat there.'

Without answering she picked up the vase of flowers taking them through to the sitting room and placing them on the occasional table.

I followed her through, hovering beside the open doorway.

'No, Benjamin, I don't think so. After all, that's Fiona's home.'

She was showing her womanly virtue, not being prepared to stray onto another female's territory.

'Fiona has her own flat,' I stated, 'it's quite close to the river at Fulham. She's let it out during her absence so as to cover the mortgage repayments.' I immediately realised I had said the wrong thing regarding Fiona's management of her financial affairs.

Returning to the kitchen, brushing past me, her reply was cryptic. 'Perhaps I should have done that, without any strings attached.'

The tone of her voice told me it was time to change the subject.

'I've got several calls to make today, various people to

see. What are you doing?'

Once again her reply was one of disinterest. 'Oh, this and that.'

By the time I had collected my briefcase from the study she had disappeared into the bathroom, the door being locked I tapped lightly on it bidding her a fond farewell.

Feeling somewhat perplexed I headed for the car. For some unknown reason her mood swing was one of disinterest towards myself. Having watched her pottering about the tiny garden and arranging flowers for the cottage, no doubt the impending sale of the cottage held a certain sadness for her.

It was early afternoon when she telephoned me on my mobile phone to say she was going away for a few days to visit her parents. A visit that was long overdue. She would be returning at the weekend.

On the Thursday evening I received a further call from her letting me know she was staying over with her parents beyond the weekend.

I was due to leave on the Monday evening on a trip to the West Country to attend a book fair, a major event in my diary. I immediately suggested that she should come with me, I would have plenty of spare time; it would be an ideal break. Her response was cool saying that all she required for the time being was her own space. Mentally kicking myself for my lack of insistence regarding matters, I replaced the receiver.

***

It was fairly late on Sunday evening when Amanda arrived, an out of the blue visit. Standing at the doorway clutching a book I had been reading I immediately invited her in, glancing beyond the open door, there was no sign of her car.

'I've just dropped my husband at the station,' she stated. 'The bloody train service is getting ridiculous, there are so many cancellations, he just hates the hassle of getting up early in the mornings to travel, so he's gone up to town this evening.'

Closing the door I led her through into the sitting room. 'I'm afraid Sally's gone away for the weekend to visit her parents. I thought you knew. Anyway, care for a drink? I take it you're not driving?'

I've left the car over at the hotel car park. We went for a meal; we usually eat out on a Sunday evening, the restaurant there is usually quiet. I can phone for a taxi, the car will be perfectly safe where it is overnight.'

My observations regarding Sally being away for the weekend had gone unanswered. I was unprepared for her visit. I had made little headway on the book I was attempting to read. The ashtray contained a mountain of cigarette butts and my glass was empty. I held the bottle up, 'Brandy all right? A civilised nightcap wouldn't you say?' She nodded.

She sipped her drink tentatively, 'Do you have any dry ginger Benjamin?'

'Yes, there must be some about here somewhere. I think it's in the drinks cabinet in the study.'

The study door being open she wandered off in that direction. I immediately followed opened the cabinet and selected the mixer drink she required, topping up her glass to the required amount.

She hovered studying the row upon row of books which were now neatly stacked on the shelves. Placing her glass on the desk she gazed about her, taking in the finely upholstered chaise longue.

'So, this is where it all happens?' Her question was somewhat ambiguous.

'Sometimes, yes. Let's go back into the sitting room.'

On her arrival my immediate thought had been that Sally had told her of the impending sale of the cottage, and the topic of conversation would revolve around this. I, in turn had deliberately not mentioned the matter. Her visit was obviously an acceptance of my previous overtures at Orchard End House during our massage session.

Having been wined and dined by her husband earlier in the evening she had arrived on my doorstep, her comment earlier in the evening of phoning for a taxi was one of female modesty and leaving her options open.

Having poured myself a drink I stood by the fireplace. She was perched on the arm of the sofa, the midi skirt she was wearing being split at the front, she was showing a provocative amount of leg.

Holding up the photograph of her from the mantelpiece for her to see, I beckoned her to my side. 'You have top billing amidst Sally's friends here. Most becoming, you riding to hounds with the local county set.'

Quickly she took it from me, 'It's ghastly; I've a good mind to confiscate it. I hate it, that's why she keeps it.'

I gave a hollow laugh, 'That's female logic for you, and look here, we have part of your outfit.' Taking up the riding crop, which hung amidst the ornamental horse brasses, I looped it around my wrist.

It was very much a replay of the overtures I had made to Sally the first morning I had been at the cottage.

Gently caressing the contours of her bottom I gave her a sharp slap.

'Ouch!'

Her response was a token cry of surprise without rejection, at the same time holding on to the riding crop, so as to avoid a further slap.

I glanced at my watch, 'Well, shall I phone for a taxi, or are you staying? I can hardly send you home to an empty house and an empty bed.'

'Don't be smug, Benjamin.' She stated my name slowly, exaggerating its pronunciation. Taking the riding crop from me she replaced it on the wall of the fireplace. 'Let's keep it straight. Nothing too heavy.'

Having spent an age in the bathroom she stood beside the bed allowing the bathrobe to fall from her revealing her naked body before slipping beneath the duvet alongside me.

I immediately manoeuvred her onto my outstretched body, as with Sally, she would be obliged to take up the dominant position. Mounting me she was turgid seeking my arousal. From beneath the pillow I produced the metal studded leather bracelets. Each had a length of chain attached to it.

She drew away from me, kneeling astride the lower part of my body. 'No, Benjamin, keep it straight.'

'Boring,' I quipped, 'this is just a variation on a theme. Give me your hands.'

Slowly she held her arms in front of me, despite her initial rejection she was warming to the situation. Having fastened the bracelets around her wrists I quickly attached the chains to the polished hardwood rail of the headboard, they were long enough to allow her plenty of freedom.

From beneath the pillow beside me I produced the riding whip, flexing it in my hands.

Wriggling and struggling against her bonds she disengaged herself from my arousal. 'No way, not that. It's bloody degrading.'

I gave her bottom a smart slap with the whip. 'You have spent far too much time in the soft caresses of another woman. So ride me well.'

'How can I when I'm tied up like this?' I guided her body into its previous position, until once again I was within her.

With her outstretched arms taking the weight of her upper body slowly she rode me. Once again flexing the whip in my hands I held it to her lips. She kissed it lightly.

'It's perfumed and it's Sally's. How often does she get the treatment?'

'Quite often, especially when she does not arrive home until the early hours of the morning. There again, you would know all about that wouldn't you? So, now it's your turn. You're a promiscuous bitch; you've scored a double. Having laid Sally in our bed, you now have me to contend with.'

She continued to rock to and fro, her eyes closed taking in the pleasure of my arousal.

The lightweight riding whip was short and perfectly balanced. With a short measured stroke I flicked the whip across her bottom. Clenching the cheeks of her bottom she whispered her contentment, 'And again.'

Ignoring her request I put the whip to her lips. Opening her eyes with lowered eyelids she kissed it, feathering it with her tongue about her lips. Teasingly I gently stroked the contours of her body with the whip. She, in turn, clenching the cheeks of her bottom in anticipation.

Suddenly altering her position she held my wrists in a vice-like grip pinning me to the bed at the same time feathering a kiss upon my lips, slowly gathering momentum her tongue penetrating my mouth. For an age she held me, smothering my mouth, her body twisting about my erection, finally her frenzy subsided, her body prone beside me she whispered, 'There you have it, girl power.'

'Is that what you call it,' I retorted, 'I like it, what happens now?'

Taking up the slack on the chains that held her to the headboard she proceeded to unfasten them. I'm going to freshen up, get dressed and phone for a taxi to take me home.'

***

Having attended the book fair, which had taken me away from home for some three days, I made an early morning dash back to the cottage arriving well before breakfast time.

I was in the process of taking my suitcase from the car when Sally appeared at the doorway.

'Oh, God, you're early,' she stated.

'Is that a problem? Do you have company?' I bantered.

Her reply was emphatic, 'No, I do not.'

'I thought Amanda might have stayed overnight.'

She stood in the doorway, her arms folded, barring my way. 'The place is a shambles. There was a party here last night. Come through to the kitchen, I'll get you a cup of coffee.'

The sitting room was littered with empty bottles and glasses; remnants of uneaten food lay on the sideboard. I duly followed her through the debris. 'Don't tell me I've missed the wake, your house-leaving party?'

Having produced two cups of coffee she sat opposite me at the breakfast bar. 'It was a hen party for one of Amanda's friends who is getting married next week. I made sure your den was strictly out of bounds so it's all clean and tidy.'

Clasping the cup in both hands she gazed at me with

large eyes. Putting aside the cup and picking up a paper table napkin, she scribbled a message, which read: I've been a bitch. Taking the pen from her, I wrote a one-word reply: AND, followed by a question mark.

'That's easy Professor, we could go to bed or do you have something else in mind?'

'First things first, Sally. Get the place clean and tidy and then we can have an early night.'

Leaning forward she peppered my face with kisses, 'You're a cruel, unkind man.'

'That's a maybe, Sally; there again I have one hell of a day in front of me. A collection of books to catalogue in readiness for sale at auction. That's why I'm back here at this unearthly hour.

***

Collecting the Mercedes from the hotel car park, I headed out from the town, negotiating the labyrinth of byways which led to the red brick mansion where I was to spend the day cataloguing the library of books in readiness for the sale of the property and its contents.

The house was buzzing with activity, a retinue of porters were busy assembling a mountain of furniture into some semblance of order. Pictures in ornate gilt frames were being carefully removed from the fine panelled walls. At the end of the day every item, from the massive four-poster bed in the master bedroom to the hotchpotch of well-worn kitchen utensils would carry its respective lot number.

I continued with the methodical task of sifting through an age-old collection of finely bound volumes.

By late afternoon the task had been completed to everybody's satisfaction. Senior members of the staff, who had travelled from London to oversee the day's operation, having delegated one of their entourage as a non-drinker for the evening to ensure a safe journey back to the capital, had invited me to join them for a drink at a local public house. The day having been a team effort, it would have been anti-social of me to refuse, although I was more than eager to get back to the cottage. Over a glass of beer the mood was convivial with much shop-talk and projected estimates of how much money the sale would realise. At the earliest opportunity however, I made my excuses to leave to return to the cottage.

Sally had certainly taken me seriously regarding making the place habitable. It was immaculate, a picture of homeliness. The remainder of the dust sheets covering the furniture had been removed, carpets vacuumed and there was a delightful aroma of lavender furniture polish. The kitchen was spotless; a vase of flowers had been placed on the breakfast bar. The fridge contained food and cans of beer.

I was making my way towards the dining room when she appeared at the top of the stairs in a shimmer of white satin pyjamas.

'Benjamin, is that you?' She came down the stairs slowly, 'I didn't hear you come in, I was in the bathroom making myself beautiful for you.'

'Pyjamas!'

'These are house pyjamas for lounging about in, not what you're thinking.'

She kissed me lightly on the cheek. The dining room furniture had been rearranged into some semblance of order. The dark oak table stood in the centre of the room. On the sideboard there was a silver tray containing glasses, bottles of scotch and gin and various mixers.

'Well, you certainly have excelled yourself, Sally.

Beer in the fridge, whisky on the sideboard and now, after a long day, a drink.'

I headed for the sideboard and poured a large measure of whisky adding a dash of soda.

'Are you having one?'

'Yes, please, a g 'n' t. A large one for Dutch courage.'

'Oh, really, that sounds ominous.' I handed her the drink. 'What have you been up to?'

From the top shelf of the sideboard she produced a piece of foolscap paper. It was a bill carrying the name of a company that supplied domestic staff to clean the homes of career females who neither had the time nor the inclination to do their own housework. I studied it at length.

'I see. What can I say, you're an idle creature, spending money without thinking.' I waved the bill in front of her, 'Dammit, you've had nothing to do all day.'

Placing her drink on the table she turned and faced me.

'What happened was this. Shortly after you left this morning Amanda called. She wanted me to help her with some shopping; apparently her husband has some VIPs coming to dinner. It was her idea to call the agency, she uses them all the time.'

'I bet she does,' I stated sardonically.

'Anyway I'm not a Mrs Mop, my talents lie elsewhere.'

Picking up her drink she stood close to me. Over the rim of her glass she pursed her lips in a pout, as a child would, knowing that she had been naughty.

'Well, Professor, it must be 'slap my wrist' time.'

Her moods were simple to understand. Addressing me as 'Professor' she had a sex game in mind, some deviant foreplay to our lovemaking.

'Yes, you could say that,' was my clipped reply. From

the living room I fetched a large silk covered cushion placing it on the table. 'Over here please.'

Putting aside her unfinished drink she stood beside the table.

'Don't be too hard on me, Benjamin.' Her voice was plaintive and childlike.

'It is a little late to be asking for leniency. You knew your duties and having spent the best part of the day with your wacky friend, it's time to pay for your misdeeds. Over you go.' Her compliance was immediate. She prostrated herself over the table, the cushion beneath her tummy; stretching her arms to their full extent she gripped the far side of the table.

Lifting one of her ankles I removed her slipper, placing it on the table. Deftly I eased the elasticated waistband of her pyjama trousers downwards to her ankles, revealing a panty girdle. Within the sheer white fabric, the rounded contours of her bottom were superb. Slowly I ran my hand over the taut, fine fabric.

'What's this? You don't need this, you have a fairly tight bum. I suppose had I left your pyjamas on this corset would have protected you from the worst of the spanking you are about to receive.'

'It's not a corset it's a body shaper. I do need it because I'm getting a bit broad in the beam. I'm very nearly size twelve now.'

As she spoke, she remained spread-eagled across the table, her face turned in my direction. I smoothed my hand over the offending garment; her breathing became measured.

'Anyway, I don't care what you do, as long as you don't send me to bed alone. That would be cruel.'

'Well, Madam, we shall see.' I tapped the backs of her thighs. 'Spread those legs.' Dutifully she obeyed.

Her legs apart, the cheeks of her bottom spread, tensing herself, the first splat of the hard-soled slipper brought an anguished gasp. Slowly and deliberately the spanking continued, the slipper held high, each cheek of her rounded buttocks being dealt with in turn as she gasped and squirmed under each stinging stroke. The final slaps being applied across the backs of her thighs. Slowly, I eased the taut sheath of her body shaper downwards until it was clear of her ankles.

'Christ, I shan't wear that again,' she gasped, 'it's worse with it on.'

'We shall see about that,' was my matter-of-fact reply. 'I rather like you in it.'

In its nakedness her bottom glowed a vivid pink. Slowly she began to rise from her undignified position.

'Stay where you are,' I ordered.

Raising her head she turned. Through the mass of her unkempt hair she faced me.

'Benjamin, you're a beast.'

Lifting her legs I replaced her satin pyjama trousers, smoothing them about her thighs. The cool fabric caressed the glowing orb of her bottom, drawing a low moan from her lips. Bending her legs she rotated her bottom as I continued to massage her through the shiny film of fabric. With a final sigh and with closed eyes she climaxed.

Having eaten very little all day and putting aside the urge to go to bed I phoned out for some food, which was promptly delivered. Savouring a can of beer surrounded by the debris of a recently finished Chinese meal, I sat on the raised brickwork of the hearth. She was sitting on the sofa opposite me, her legs tucked beneath her.

In a low, barely audible voice, she spoke. 'That's your favourite corner isn't it?' The place you headed for the first evening you came.'

I nodded my head in agreement. In the subdued light her eyes appeared moist, a hint of tears upon her cheeks.

'What's the matter, Sally? You're crying.'

'They're nothing tears, it's not important. I've got pins and needles.' Slowly she unfolded her legs, stretching them out fully so that they rested on the low occasional table that stood between us.

Putting aside the plates and cutlery I sat on the table cradling her feet on my lap, gently rubbing them.

'Is it Amanda? What has she said about our arrangement? I assume you've exchanged confidences.'

'She's happy.' Wriggling her toes, she giggled. 'She likes you, and now you have the two of us.'

Inwardly I knew her flippancy was to cover her conflict of emotions. Her tears were hybrid tears of both joy and sadness, the kind of tears shed by middle-aged women at weddings for reasons known only to themselves.

One did not need the expertise of a psychoanalyst to understand their coming together. From snippets of gossip I gathered that Amanda's first marriage had been a disaster, as was Sally's relationship with her interior designer.

As an active bi-sexual, Amanda had found security with a man many years her senior; with Sally in tow she had all that she could wish for.

Slowly she eased her legs away from my lap, standing up. 'You brought me off earlier with the slipper, take me to bed for lots of cuddles. Screw me in the morning.'

***

Across the fields the outline of numerous marquees could be seen. White blotches interspersed with coloured pennants and bunting. It was the day of the town's summer fête, an annual event organised by the local Chamber of

Trade. I had been dragooned into giving my services; a marquee had been set up where people could bring items of bric-a-brac and family heirlooms to have them valued. For this they would be obliged to make a small donation.

Sporting a lapel badge, which gave me free entry into the ground, I had been chided unmercifully by Sally. Earlier in the morning there had been a telephone call from Amanda. Apparently, her husband had been delegated as one of the panel of judges who would judge the various carnival floats that would parade through the town. However, he had been delayed in town on some urgent business or other and therefore she would be taking his place.

Sally's outfit for the afternoon was a simple summer dress and a wide-brimmed straw hat with a pair of sensible sandals. She stated that for the afternoon she would be doing her own thing, no doubt joining up with a few of the regulars that frequented the Maltings wine bar.

My stint at the antique valuation marquee was somewhat uneventful. Although many people brought in items of porcelain, silver and furniture to be valued, my department of books, prints and ancient maps did not feature as very collectable to them.

Mid-afternoon found me heading for the refreshment tent, a small marquee that had been designated for the use of officials only.

Amanda was there in deep conversation with a matronly, middle-aged female. She was dressed in a pair of high-waisted, cream coloured trousers, well cut so as not to accentuate her full hips. The top she wore was black and sleeveless, her wide brimmed hat was trimmed with a wide, scarlet ribbon.

Ordering a beer I drank it from the bottle standing some distance away, manoeuvring myself so that the person she was in conversation with had her back to me. I pointed my finger to the top of my head, silently mouthing the words of the well-known, somewhat smutty adage, "red hat, no drawers". Her lip reading was perfect. She shook her head slowly from side to side. Within a few minutes she had joined me kissing me lightly on the cheek. Her perfume was subtle, yet delightfully heady.

Casting my eyes over her from head to toe, I stated, 'You're the perfect picture of a diplomat's wife.'

'Stop taking the piss. Where's Sally?' She had adopted one of Sally's mannerisms of using crude invective in a sophisticated tone of voice.

'She's doing her own thing this afternoon, freelancing, so to speak. I did catch sight of her earlier on posing about the place, sickening to watch. And you without your husband. Will you be at the disco this evening? More important, who will be sharing your bed, or is he due home later in the day? I hate to think of you being alone.'

Momentarily my questions went unanswered. Taking her cigarettes from her handbag she lit one. 'Do I have a choice?'

I ignored the question. 'How did you get here?'

'By car of course. That's why I'm drinking mineral water.'

Let's go back to Orchard End, now that Sally's sold the cottage surely you're going to allow me a final fling so to speak, and then tonight when you have danced the night away at the village hop, I'm sure Sally will be pleased to stay overnight with you. I'm going to have another drink, how about you?'

She nodded her head slowly. 'I'll stick with the same please.'

By the time I had returned with the drinks she was sitting at a table.

'If we're going back to my place I don't want anything too heavy, keep it straight and simple.'

I savoured my drink, it was a strong continental lager and I was on my third bottle. My inhibitions had been cast aside; I sat down beside her.

'I'd like to spread you naked over some bales of straw and screw you.'

A smile feathered her lips. 'Bloody uncomfortable I should say. You really are the pits aren't you? That's a kink of yours is it? The urge to do it amid the dust and muck of some outbuilding?'

Sally's revelation during our early morning pillow talk some days previously, of Amanda's interest in one of the erotic cameo items they had read together which took place at a riding stable, the female participant being chastised for her waywardness, had set me thinking.

'Not too heavy, straight and simple, you say. Not quite what I had in mind.'

From my jacket pocket I produced the photograph, now devoid of its frame, of her in her horse riding finery. Hurriedly scribbling a note on the back of it, I placed it on the table. 'See you in about an hour.'

Immaculate in her riding outfit she stood amidst the dust and grime of the attic room above the stables, which had once been the groom's quarters. I had chosen the longest riding crop; it was fine and pliant, tapering to a fine, feathered tip.

'You can leave your breeches on,' I stated. 'Should I mark your bottom your husband would wish to know how it came about. But there again, you very rarely share his bed, but one cannot be too careful.'

She removed her soft leather gloves, handing them to me.

'Take off your hat and jacket.' Slowly she obeyed my command. 'Your hairstyle is far too formal, unpin it.'

Once again, looking me straight in the eye, she obeyed. As her arms reached upwards, her breasts stood proud beneath her cream coloured blouse. The task completed she shook her head, her hair falling to her shoulders. Handing me the hairpins I placed them in her riding hat. I allowed her black velvet riding jacket to fall to the floor amidst the dust and fragments of straw, placing her riding hat on top.

'Christ, Benjamin, that's bloody expensive clobber. Find a place to hang them up.'

I ignored her request. 'Put your hands on the top of your head.'

'Now I will finish the job.' I removed the fine jewelled clasp from her chiffon scarf, placing it on the window sill, which was thick with dust and covered by a multitude of dead insects. There was a look of disapproval as she glanced sideways in my direction. Slowly I undid the scarf, gently removing it from her neck, allowing it to drift slowly to the floor. In a slow, methodical manner I unfastened the buttons of her blouse, revealing her bra and bare tummy. I could sense the increased rhythm of her breathing, the gentle up and down movement of her breasts as I carried out the task.

'Hands down by your sides, please.'

I undid the wrist buttons; walking behind her I eased the blouse downwards to the floor. Deftly I unfastened her bra; it was immaculate, crisp and white; this too, fell to the floor. With the tip of the riding crop I flicked the garments across the dusty floor into a crumpled heap.

She remained upright and waiting naked from the waist up, her hands on her head, her annoyance was obvious.

Earlier, amidst the clutter of jumble in the room, I had found a crude timber trestle that had obviously been used at some time as a stand for the cleaning of saddles. It was virtually made to measure for my requirements; a ready-made bench. Placing a horse blanket on the top rail, I gave my orders.

'Over you go.'

Slowly she bent over the trestle, her rump high as she placed her delicate, manicured hands flat down on the grimy floor, she grimaced. I gave her raised bottom a sharp stroke of the whip.

'Kindly don't show your petulance, madam.'

'Bastard,' she snapped.

'That one word has just earned you three extra strokes,' I retorted. 'You're a spirited filly and I intend to school you well.'

Taking a wide leather strap, part of some discarded riding tack, I slipped it under the bar of the trestle and around her waist. This would restrict her from attempting to rise during her punishment. I tapped the heels of her highly polished riding boots.

'Spread, please.' She eased her legs further apart.

'Now madam, I will dust your ample bottom.'

She was looking sideways at me through a mass of unkempt hair, her face glared defiance. Standing at the correct distance I applied the whip slowly, after each stroke I smoothed the contours of her bottom. The material of her riding breeches being fairly thick, the strokes were severe. As each stroke fell she bit her lip in anguish. Her punishment completed, I unfastened the leather strap from around her waist.

Slowly and painfully, she drew herself upright, clutching her bottom, rubbing it vigorously. She turned to face me, her once impeccable make-up a sorry sight. Her naked upper torso flecked with dust, her clothing a crumpled heap upon the floor, I pointed the whip towards them.

Slowly she bent over picking them up one by one, shaking the dust and fragments of straw from them, before folding them over her arm.

'You're a mess,' I stated. 'I suggest you take a shower.'

We made our way down the narrow stairway through the barn to the changing room. Without saying a word she walked in front of me. I had the feeling that the degradation of her chastisement at my hands hurt her deeply.

Unbuttoning her riding breeches she eased them down to the top of her riding boots to reveal a black panty girdle. Sitting on the slatted pine bench she struggled to take off her riding boots.

'Can you fetch some towels from the cupboard beside the sauna cabin, please Benjamin.'

The tone of her voice hovered between being contrite, yet somehow assertive. By the time I had returned with the towels and a bathrobe she had undressed.

We entered the shower together, a fine spray of water fell about us. I sponged her bottom and her breasts with herbal body gel before guiding her hands to my penis. Under the warm cascade of water she appeared non-receptive, almost brittle. I continued to soap her bottom and between her legs before guiding my penis within her. For some time she twisted and rotated the lower part of her body.

'We are going to bed, aren't we?'

I nodded my head. 'Of course.'

By the time she had finished drying herself I was fully dressed. Barefoot in the afternoon sunshine, wearing nothing but her bathrobe, with her clothes tucked under her arm, she tiptoed her way across the gravel driveway to the cool comfort of the house.

The kitchen was large but cosy, with a low-beamed ceiling. There was an Aga cooker housed within a massive chimney breast. At the far end of the room a window looked out onto the walled kitchen garden. The kitchen table was of antique pine, surrounded by Windsor chairs.

From the fridge she produced a bottle of white wine.

'Perhaps you would like to do the honours. Glasses and a corkscrew, bottom shelf of the dresser.'

As I poured the wine she folded her riding gear. 'There's one helluva cleaning bill here, wouldn't you say?' Ignoring her remarks I tasted the wine before handing her a glass. She sipped it, running the tip of her tongue along her lips. 'How often does Sally get the treatment?'

'You wouldn't expect me to divulge our bedtime intimacies, would you? What makes you think she does?'

'I've seen the tell-tale marks on her tight little bottom on more than one occasion.'

She held the black panty girdle in front of her as if to examine it for any blemishes.

'Wearing a foundation garment, was that Sally's suggestion? I assume she telephoned you before my arrival?'

'No. Under the circumstances it was the appropriate garment to wear, it served its purpose, except for a couple of times when you caught me low down.'

I took the garment from her, at the same time unfastening her bathrobe so that it fell open. She stood seemingly transfixed, lowering her hand to cover her pubis. I held my glass to her lips for her to drink. She sipped it slowly, once again feathering her tongue about her lips. I lowered the glass, dipping my fingers into the pale yellow liquid. Gently I moistened the pink cones of her nipples with the wine, leaning forward licking the moistness. I repeated the operation, gently sucking each nipple in turn, nuzzling her cleavage. She took the glass from me placing it on the table.

'You're a tit and bum person, aren't you?'

I nodded. 'It's time we went to bed, otherwise we shall be stood here all afternoon.'

Once again she wrapped her bathrobe about her body tying the belt loosely about her waist before heading off across the kitchen to a narrow doorway. I followed carrying the bottle of wine and glasses. The door opened to reveal a narrow, steep stairway. I waited until she had reached the top before following.

The bedroom was surprisingly large, no doubt some time in the dim and distance past, it had housed more than one servant girl. The décor was ultra-feminine; it was obviously their love nest. The centre of the room being taken up by a clumsy bed of brass and matt ironwork, an item of trendy fashion in the world of home décor. It was smothered in rosebud bed linen.

She stood in front of a pine chest of drawers, which was topped by an angled mirror, which gave a perfect reflection of the bed. A blanket box of pale green wickerwork with a buttoned velvet top stood at the base of the bed. Slipping out of my casual lightweight jacket, I hung it on the bedpost. She had turned to face me, leaning back on the chest of drawers.

'Don't be shy, come over here. You said it was to be strictly a one-off session, so let's make the most of it.'

The brass metalwork at the foot of the bed was lower than that of the headboard. Taking a pillow I placed it over the top rail, easing the blanket box away from the bed by a few inches. I sat on the blanket box, taking off my shoes and trousers. I lowered the bathrobe from her shoulders so that she stood naked.

'Don't go cold on me now, over here.'

Slowly she knelt on the blanket box, bending over, her tummy resting on the pillow, her arms outstretched, her hands resting on the bed.

'Please Benjamin, no more whipping.'

'I shall give you something I suspect you haven't had for some time, although I understand you are a well broken filly in this department. I shall cork your bum. You have a fine horse riding bottom, it's just beautiful.'

Taking a tube of lubricant jelly from my jacket pocket and easing her legs wide apart, I fingered the silken smooth gel into the crevice of her bottom. Gently breaking within her, her hands clutching the bed cover as I entered. Gripping her waist I held her to me, my erection held in a pulsing velvet vice. In a wave of elation I eased to and fro. The sighing of her orgasm was unreal, a sobbing crescendo. The window of the bedroom being open, no doubt the crying of her ecstasy could have been heard beyond the house. All too soon I had succumbed, spent within her.

Covered by a lightweight bedspread we lay on the bed. Beyond the open window I could hear the sounds of birdsong. Eventually, she spoke.

'Had you found Sally in bed with some randy sales rep the other day, I suppose you would have spent the afternoon packing up your precious collection of books before disappearing with your tail between your legs?'

'Don't spoil the moment, let's just lay here and listen to the sounds of summer, it's beautiful. Anyway, what would you do if you found Sally in bed with another woman?'

Her answer was one of mock possessiveness, 'I'd scratch her eyes out.'

'No you wouldn't, you're not a fully-fledged dike, just

a creature of ambiguous gender. By taking a female lover you can hardly be accused of being unfaithful to your husband. After all, your body isn't being plundered by some illicit penis.'

Raising her head, laying on her side, she turned to face me. 'Christ, you say the weirdest things.'

'Think about it. How many wives lie in bed at night straddled by an overweight, insensitive partner, pandering to his needs with a fake orgasm, faithful in the flesh but emotionally fantasising?'

My observations went unanswered. 'I suspect your emotional involvement with Sally stemmed from her vulnerability. I gather the last man in her life was nothing but an upper-bracket waster.'

'You can say that again. He was nothing but a prize prat. After they split, in a strange kind of way she was inconsolable. She went absolutely wild; together we did the rounds at some way-out, swinging parties. I think she took me along as a kind of chaperon. By the end of the night every room we happened to go into was full of people fucking, blokes together, three in a bed, you name it... really OTT. You know how it is with theatrical people.'

Reaching out across my prone body to the bedside table she poured herself a glass of wine, sipping it slowly, licking her lips. 'It's gone a little tepid.'

I eased myself into a sitting position sampling the wine. 'Yes, never mind.'

As she lay back on the bed I manoeuvred her body so that she lay on her tummy. Burying her face in the pillow with her arms outstretched she gripped the vertical bars of the headboard. Pulling aside the bedspread I gently massaged the contours of her shoulders, her back and bottom.

'Stay as you are, your Freudian slip is showing. I like your self-imposed bondage.'

Wriggling her bottom she answered me. 'Just pandering to your needs.'

She was becoming girly, almost coquettish. I gave her bottom a hard slap with the palm of my hand.

Wriggling sideways she gathered the bedspread about her naked body, rolling over to the edge of the bed. 'I'm getting out of here before you start laying into me again.'

Once clear of the bed she threw the bedspread in my direction.

From the wardrobe she selected a frock to wear, disappearing in the direction of the en-suite bathroom.

It was some considerable time before she returned wearing a two-piece sundress. Through the fine fabric her breasts were beautifully displayed. Womanhood in full bloom.

'Feel free to use the bathroom, Benjamin.' Picking up the glass of wine she sipped it slowly. 'Now that I am all aglow and beautiful, I think I deserve another treat.'

'Really, what do you have in mind?'

'I'd like Sally to stay the night.'

'I shall have to think about that, I haven't finished with her for this afternoon's escapade.'

'Not today, Benjamin, leave it, you've had me, you've had your fix for the day, there's always tomorrow.'

***

That evening found me at an old people's bungalow on a Council estate in one of the outlying villages. The elderly lady resident had approached me earlier in the day enquiring whether I would be interested in purchasing some books that had belonged to her late husband, hence my visit.

He had been a gamekeeper on a large country estate. On his retirement they were obliged to leave their country cottage and had been allocated the bungalow.

The room held the faded memorabilia of his life, the walls being festooned with faded sepia photos of country house shooting parties. Masses of dead game birds proudly laid out to signify a successful day's shoot.

A small glass-fronted bookcase held the collection of some fifty or sixty books of country house living in a bygone age. In a moment of spontaneous philanthropy I selected a collection of six finely-bound volumes, offering her £250 for them, which she readily accepted. Excited and overcome by the sum of money a few paltry books had brought her, she insisted I had a glass of sherry. The £250 would enable her to visit her daughter and grandchildren, who lived some distance away.

Heading homewards I stopped at a country pub. Over a pint of mediocre mild ale I reflected on the day's happenings. Inwardly I knew I should not have invaded Amanda and Sally's love sanctum.

The road back to town took me past Orchard End. Stopping the car at the entrance of the driveway, I cast my eyes over the house. Sally's car was parked close by the house, a pale light shone from the open bedroom window, a wisp of lace curtaining fluttering in the breeze had caught on a climbing rose bush, which clung to the wall of the building. I sat, seemingly transfixed, in my mind's eye I could imagine their soft embraces, the muted turmoil of their togetherness. Spent and beautiful they would sleep cocooned in the aftermath of their lovemaking.

For myself, the afternoon intake of alcohol, followed by the torrid 'no-holds barred' foray to Orchard End House with Amanda, had been an obvious reaction to the faxed message I had received from Fiona the previous day.

A cryptic out-of-the-blue announcement that she would be returning to the UK, arriving at Heathrow, the following morning. The message had ended with an emphatic request that I should be there to meet her...